THE MAJOR'S BRIDE

Coming to the door, Roderick watched Elizabeth as she walked among the wildflowers in the meadow. Her thick brown hair sparkled with golden glints in the morning sun as she stooped to pluck a daisy. She reminded him of an elusive wood nymph that might escape him if he weren't careful.

Pushing such fanciful thoughts from his mind, he strode to where she stood with her back to him. "Miss Fields, we must speak before the others return."

Elizabeth looked at him with shuttered blue eyes. Her tone was polite, but decidedly cool. "Major Shelton, I must thank you for your protection during this harrowing event."

Her manner was not encouraging, but Roderick persisted. "Miss Fields . . . Elizabeth, I must tell you that your kiss—"

"Sir, don't be so unkind as to remind me." Elizabeth gave a brittle laugh as she looked away from him. "I was very frightened when the candle went out, and you must attribute my actions to that. I hold you under no obligation . . ."

Roderick, losing patience with Elizabeth's cool demeanor, grasped her by the shoulders, turning her to face him. He wanted to kiss her again until she was breathless, but her face was a mask of icy composure. He suspected he was making a mess of this proposal. "The circumstances, my dear, are not to be ignored. You can be certain that no one else will disregard the fact that we have been out here in each other's company all night. Elizabeth, you *must* marry me. . . ."

ROMANCE

# WATCH FOR THESE REGENCY ROMANCES

# ELIZABETH AND THE MAJOR

## Lynn Collum

Zebra Books
Kensington Publishing Corp.
http://www.zebrabooks.com

ZEBRA BOOKS are published by

Kensington Publishing Corp.
850 Third Avenue
New York, NY 10022

Zebra and the Z logo Reg. U.S. Pat. & TM Off.

First Printing: August, 1997
10 9 8 7 6 5 4 3 2 1

Printed in the United States of America

*For my friends
Connie Fowler, Helene Radjeski, and Tina Estep.
Thanks for all you do.*

# One

"Lizzie, Lizzie, Papa wishes to see you in the library as soon as you are finished here," the youngest daughter of the vicar of Aylsham exclaimed as she dashed into the kitchen in search of her eldest sister.

Never taking her eyes from the flowers in the Wedgwood vase, Miss Elizabeth Fields placed another rose in the arrangement, then addressed her sibling as she eyed the effect. "Dearest, how many times must I tell you that young ladies do not run?"

"But you don't understand. This is quite urgent, for you are to go on a journey." Ruth tugged at her sister's arm.

At last turning to look down at the girl, Elizabeth noted the excitement shining in the child's blue eyes. "We are to embark on a trip?"

"Not we, only you, Lizzie. I heard Papa talking to Lady Powers as he walked her to her carriage."

"Perhaps you misunderstood." Elizabeth frowned as she removed her gloves and untied the apron which was protecting her blue sprig muslin gown. How could she leave with her brothers returning home this very week?

"No, 'tis Sarah that is forever getting things mixed up. I tell you Papa said you would accompany Julia since Lady Powers must stay with Edward. She said he is covered head to toe in red spots." Ruth giggled her delight at young Lord Powers's condition. She thought that one who so often tormented the Fields sisters should now suffer for his villainy.

Picking up the vase and exiting the kitchen, Elizabeth teased, "Will you think it so funny should you and Sarah come down with the measles?"

Ruth dashed past her sister into the hall and stood on tiptoe to look in the gilt-framed mirror. Like all the Fields, she was blessed with dark brown curls, striking blue eyes, and a handsome countenance. The idea of being covered with red spots horrified her. "Lizzie, I see one! A red spot on my nose!"

"Since you have not been in company with Edward in over a month, I should very much doubt you are contracting the illness." Elizabeth placed the vase on a console table below the mirror, turning the arrangement to find the best view.

"Look, right here on my nose." Ruth pointed at a faint reddish mark.

Elizabeth looked closely, then began to shake her head. "Just as I thought. You are getting freckles from not wearing your bonnet."

Without saying a word, the child spun on her heel and dashed to the stairs. As she mounted the first step she saw her sister's raised eyebrow. Straightening her back, Ruth slowed her pace to a sedate walk.

Elizabeth's mouth twitched as she watched the seven-year-old ascend the stairs as regally as a duchess. "Where are you going, my dear?"

"To soak my face in Denmark Lotion. Sarah's magazine says all the ladies use it for their complexions." So saying, the child marched up to the room she shared with her sister.

Suspecting she would be called upon in a matter of minutes to intervene in an argument between her two younger siblings, Elizabeth decided to discover what her father wanted. She softly tapped on the library door, then entered when she heard the vicar's voice.

"Good morning, Papa. Ruth tells me you wished to speak with me."

The Reverend Mr. Percy Fields rose from his chair, gesturing for his daughter to take the seat before his desk. "Yes, Elizabeth. You are in looks today, my dear. How you remind me of your dear mother."

Elizabeth dismissed the flattery as a father's partiality for his child, for despite her beauty she'd been taught to value more important qualities like kindness and loyalty. She settled into the chair and resisted the urge to straighten the clutter of books and papers upon his desk.

The vicar removed his glasses and laid them on the open Bible he'd been using to prepare his sermon. He then took a seat and frowned as he dropped into silence while he contemplated his daughter.

His dear friend, Miss Lilian Wade, was right. Elizabeth had lost that sparkle in her eyes that was always so much a part of her. Was he to blame? Had he allowed his eldest daughter to shoulder too many of his responsibilities for the family? He continued to brood for some minutes about his culpability.

As her father's silence lengthened, Elizabeth admired his countenance. He was a handsome man, with his gentle blue eyes and his dark hair showing only a hint of grey at the temples. Fate had dealt him an unkind blow by taking his wife so young. Elizabeth had done all in her power to ease his burden by taking charge of her four younger siblings, a task which left her with little time for herself. But she loved her family dearly and did not think the cost too dear.

Her father cleared his throat, as if he had some momentous thing to say. "Well, my dear, I had a visit from Lady Powers. She brought the most amazing news. Your dear friend, Julia, is invited north to Langley Hall next week by a distant cousin."

"That is wonderful news, Papa. Julia could use some time away from Riverview." What Elizabeth really meant was time away from Lady Powers, but she would never say such an unkind thing in front of Papa.

" 'Tis more than a mere invitation, Lizzie. Her cousin, having never married, is looking for a beneficiary for her fortune and estates. Miss Powers, along with several other relatives, is being considered for that role. The future recipient of the fortune will reside permanently with Miss Langley henceforth."

"Why, Papa, that is the best news I have heard in an age." Elizabeth clasped her hands together. Having known Julia since they were both in leading strings, Elizabeth knew that her friend deserved a life away from the cold and domineering Lady Powers.

"Yes, very fortuitous for Miss Powers, if she is the one selected. But with Edward still recovering from his illness and Lady Powers's own sister unable to travel with the girl, the baroness has requested that you accompany Julia to Harrowgate." Seeing his daughter frown, the vicar leaned forward with a rush of words. "Elizabeth, I hope you will agree to go, for I think Julia needs your support."

"Papa, how can I leave you with Cook gone to visit her ailing sister and only Becky to help handle everything? Both John and Matthew return this week and the house will be at sixes and sevens. As much as I should like to go for my friend's sake, 'tis not to be considered." Elizabeth shook her head, but she felt a twinge of regret, for she would dearly love a visit to some country estate where there would be new friends to be met.

"Lady Powers has thought of that, my dear. She said that while her sister is not up to the long journey with her niece, Miss Lilian will take your place here while you are away. The short ride from Riverview to Aylsham will not be too great for the lady. 'Tis the movement of a carriage that makes her ill just like our Sarah." Still seeing the frown on his daughter's face, the vicar added, "My dear, I believe Julia needs you, and I am certain we shall survive for so short a time. Say you will go."

Mr. Fields watched his daughter closely. It was wrong that she was sacrificing her youth in helping him with the children. But he'd been so taken with her settled behavior after she had taken up her duties that he'd allowed her to continue at the post. The care-for-nothing young girl, who'd dashed about the county helter-skelter, had suddenly become a pattern card of propriety after the death of her mother.

They'd been in mourning on Elizabeth's eighteenth birthday, and so she'd missed the long-planned visit to London for a Season. Each year since, Mr. Fields had attempted to arrange another chance for his daughter, but she wouldn't hear of such. He'd been surprised, for while she had been vastly fond of riding and dancing before his wife's death, once assuming the mantle of responsibility for their household, Lizzie had rejected the proposed trip to London vehemently. She'd proven amazingly strong willed on the subject.

Three years had passed since Norma Fields had died and the vicar, now that the matter had been pointed out, was honest enough to admit that he'd unfairly taken advantage of his dear Lizzie. She'd been the one to keep the household running when he was too sunken in grief to care.

As he'd come to accept his loss, Mr. Fields had made modest efforts to refocus his daughter's energies, but she'd been unyielding in giving up what she saw as her duty. Now, Lady Powers had presented him the perfect opportunity to make Elizabeth think about her own needs for a change. This trip was an enticement which he hoped she couldn't resist. It would fulfill her need to be helpful, and she would have some time away from the drudgery of managing the family. He hoped she wouldn't merely go with Julia but would have a grand time as well.

Feeling her father's hopeful gaze resting on her, Elizabeth rose and walked to the window. She was torn. She knew that Julia would need her support and friendship. In truth it would be far better for Elizabeth to accompany her friend than Julia's mother, for Lady Powers was forever finding fault with her only daughter.

The question foremost in Elizabeth's mind was, could Miss Wade truly handle this very active household? Julia's aunt was a spinster nearing her fourth decade, and, much like her niece, was shy and unassuming. Elizabeth liked the lady excessively and often lamented the fact that Lilian Wade was little better than an unpaid servant at Riverview.

The thought suddenly occurred that Julia's aunt might just welcome the time away from Lady Power's residence, and if her friend truly needed her . . .

"Very well, Papa. I shall go with Julia and do all I can to see her settled as the heiress. But should you find that Miss Lilian is not up to the task, promise you will send word at once."

"I promise, my dear."

The clatter of footsteps sounded on the stairs in the hall before the door to the library flew open. Twelve-year-old Miss Sarah Fields stood with arms akimbo, her dark blue eyes glittering with outrage. "Lizzie, you must tell Ruth that she cannot use all my Denmark Lotion on a single freckle."

"Is that the proper way to enter a room?" Elizabeth asked distractedly. Her mind was already on ways to aid Julia to make a favorable impression on her possible benefactress.

"Oh, I am sorry, Papa." Sarah sketched a curtsey for her smiling father. "Ruth makes me so angry that I forget myself. You must stop her before she wastes the entire bottle that my friend, Mariah, sent me."

Elizabeth realized she must handle the current crisis before worrying about Julia. She smiled at her father as she turned her sister back towards the door. "Come, I shall see what can be done to save your precious lotion. We must leave Papa in peace or he shall never get his sermon prepared. With no sermon to give, he might end up with no parish *and* a set of freckled-faced daughters."

Mr. Fields heard Sarah laugh as the door closed. He was glad Elizabeth would accompany her friend to Langley Hall. Hopefully, the stubborn miss would at last be convinced that he could manage things quite well without her. The problem was, she seemed determined to remain at her post until Ruth and Sarah were grown and married. At one-and-twenty Elizabeth was already considered a spinster by the local ladies.

His beautiful Lizzie a spinster. No, he would not have that. He hoped while his daughter was away she might meet a worthy gentleman to whom she'd take a liking. Then he realized that was a fanciful thought. More likely her visit to Langley Hall would be merely a much deserved respite from her onerous tasks, and she would return more determined than ever to do what she saw as her duty.

Perchance while his daughter was away, he would make changes at the vicarage. He wasn't certain how, he only knew Lizzie was too beautiful and good to have put all thoughts of marriage behind her. Perhaps Miss Wade could offer some advice during her stay. He would seek her help. She was such a wise and sensitive lady.

"I am to leave school?" Miss Imogene Shelton started from her chair, her face alight with excitement as she looked to Miss Johnson, the headmistress of the Johnson

Seminary for Young Ladies. When the lady nodded her head in the affirmative, Imogene turned to her half brother, Major Roderick Shelton. He stood beside the fireplace, erect and handsome in his red uniform. There was no visible evidence of the wound he'd received two months before at the storming of Badajoz, since he no longer required the use of a cane.

"Then I am to have a Season after all. Uncle Matthew has agreed to my coming to London."

Roderick frowned. " 'Twas never a question of what Viscount Kirtland agreed to. The sticking point has been Miss Johnson's reports of your conduct."

Imogene blushed and flashed an irritated glance at her teacher before stating her case to her brother. " 'Tis only that I am the oldest girl still at school. I am terribly bored. I cannot see that taking a ride with Martha Worthingham's brother was such a great offense. Oh, Roderick, he had a high-perched phaeton and—"

"*And* you were seen riding unaccompanied by half the residents of Bath—at an indecorous speed." Roderick shook his head, but he did not pursue the matter further. "I have already spoken on that topic as much as I wish. I have come today to take you to Harrowgate."

"Harrowgate!" The disgust was evident in Imogene's tone. "Another watering hole for the aged and the infirm. Am I never to have any chance to meet eligible young men?"

"Miss Shelton," Miss Johnson snapped primly, "if you would but give your brother a chance, he would explain your good fortune to you."

"Perhaps I might speak to my sister in private, Miss Johnson." Roderick felt that the teacher, with her censuring tone, was only antagonizing his half sister.

"Yes, Major. I think that might be for the best." The headmistress shot Imogene a warning look to be on her best behavior, then exited the small room.

Roderick's sister stood beside a round cloth-covered table fingering one of the dozens of miniatures of former students which cluttered the small room, a sulky look clouding her pretty face. She was very much a stranger to him, for he had placed her under Miss Johnson's care after her mother died some seven years ago. His infrequent visits were not due to lack of affection on his part, but due to having to earn his living as a soldier, for his late father had been a mere younger son who'd inherited only a small income which had ceased at his death.

"Genie," he said, using his old childhood name for her. "Don't look as if all is lost. You have known for years that the viscount never intended to aid either of us." Roderick never referred to the man as his uncle, for the gentleman had never treated them like family.

"But I don't understand. You are his heir. How can he not wish us to visit him occasionally?" Imogene set the picture back upon the table and went to her brother, placing a hand tenderly upon his arm. " 'Tis not fair to you."

"I think he is quite determined that his brother's son shall not inherit. I believe he never got over my mother choosing our father over him. He has recently informed me, through his solicitor, that he is engaged to be married."

"Then we must find some lady of good fortune for *you* to marry."

Roderick's green eyes narrowed and hardened. "Do you forget that I *was* once engaged to be married and it proved to be a disaster? I have no intention of ever entering into a betrothal again."

"But you cannot judge all women by Miss Martin. Even I could see that she was a vain and shallow creature. I am glad she eloped with that Irish baronet, for she was not a fit wife for a soldier."

"That is the crux of the problem, Genie. Soldiers

should not marry, for they must invariably leave their wives for long periods of time or bring them along to follow the drum. Either way, it is a very hard life for a female. I was a fool last year to even have considered marriage. I shall never again ask a lady to do choose such a life."

Home on leave the year before, the major had quickly become enchanted with a dark-haired Bath beauty and, against his usual habits, had rashly offered for her. He had never admitted it to anyone but himself, but his be-trothed's betrayal had scarcely affected him, for he'd quickly determined she had little to offer but a pretty face. She'd proven to be an excessively spoiled lady who'd become furious when he returned to his unit instead of continuing to dance attendance on her. She would have made life a misery for both him and his sister. But the incident reaffirmed the notion he'd long held that sol-diers should never marry.

Imogene's shoulders sagged. "Then you have only your military pay to support us. I am sorry I have plagued you so about going to Town. I shall go to Harrowgate and be frugal."

Impulsively, Roderick bent down and kissed his half sis-ter's cheek. Despite her headstrong nature, she had a kind heart. "Don't look so glum. You are to go to Har-rowgate, but not to live in genteel poverty. Miss Johnson received a letter from a distant relative of your mother's. She has invited you to Langley Hall, some ten miles from the town, for she is to select one of her relatives to be her beneficiary."

"You mean I might become an heiress?" Imogene's face lit at the prospect.

"I should very much like you to be comfortably settled before I return to my unit. If a fortune goes with that, all the better. But, Imogene, you cannot be chasing after every young man with a fine carriage, or acting the hoyden at Langley Hall, and expect to be chosen to inherit her legacy. Miss Esmé Langley will be looking for a genteel young lady to whom she might bequeath her estate."

"Hoyden! I am no such thing." Imogene flounced away from her brother, going to stare out the tall window at the traffic on Sidney Place. As her gaze was drawn to a shining blue phaeton across the street, she could not refute her weakness for dashing young men with sporting vehicles.

Roderick grew restless as his sister stood with her back to him. He had no wish to catalogue the tales which had come to him through letters from Miss Johnson. He thought another tack would be better. "Perhaps you might model your behavior after one of your teachers here at school while we are there."

Imogene turned and give him a false smile. "Oh, truly I can simper and toad-eat just like Miss Johnson when the mood takes me."

Roderick sighed. He could not deny that Miss Johnson at times did both. "Then I suggest you search your memory and use your own mother as a model for proper behavior, for she was my idea of the perfect lady—quiet, gentle, accommodating, and, most of all, aware of the proprieties one must follow."

The mocking look dropped from Imogene's face. "Yes, Mama was all that I would wish to be." Hurrying to her brother, she threw herself into his arms. "I shall be on my best behavior, dearest Roderick, I promise. And when I am an heiress, you may come and live with me; then I shall no longer have to fear your ever being wounded again."

The major stroked his sister's red hair as he held her. He was determined to help her gain the Langley legacy. It would assure her a place in Society and a female relative to look after her. He could then return to his regiment without the constant worry of what would happen to her should he die fighting the French.

Despite her plans for him to stay with her, he knew that he would not be comfortable living off another's good fortune. He was heir to a viscount, but with his uncle's impending marriage, Roderick knew he could never borrow against his expectations. He had chosen the military, and that was the life to which he would return once he had Imogene safely settled in Yorkshire.

The large old traveling carriage rumbled north along the road from Harrowgate. Despite its ancient design, Lady Powers had made certain that the lacquered surface and the brass lanterns and fittings of the coach had been polished to perfection. Her efforts, however, had been in vain, for the carriage was now covered in road dust.

Ensconced in the faded luxury of the interior, Elizabeth and Julia sat in the comfortable silence of long acquaintance. Accompanying the ladies was a young maid named Margie who sat quietly with her back to the horses, enjoying her first trip away from Riverview.

At a distance, one might have mistaken Miss Powers and Miss Fields for sisters, their colouring being quite similar. But upon closer inspection, the girls were different in both looks and temperament.

While Elizabeth was blessed with mahogany brown hair that curled naturally around an arrestingly beautiful oval face, Julia's hair was a shade lighter and had to be crimped into fashionable curls. The vicar's daughter had sparkling blue eyes framed by dark lashes, a dainty nose, and a full rosy mouth most often set in a cheerful smile. The baroness's daughter had eyes more grey than blue, giving her an aloof look; her nose was a trifle too long; and her mouth, while well shaped, was often puckered in worry. But despite their differences the young ladies had forged a lasting friendship which was devoid of rivalry or jealousy.

Elizabeth watched as Julia distractedly twisted the ribbons, which hung down the front of her yellow traveling dress, around her slender fingers. It was an old habit from her childhood, and the gesture alerted Elizabeth to how nervous Julia was about the coming meeting with her unknown relative.

Thinking to draw out her friend, she casually inquired, "You did not tell me just how you are related to Miss Langley. I don't believe I have ever heard you or your mother mention the lady."

"As to that, I did not know of her existence until the letter arrived. Mama said she is a distant cousin of my father's, but she could not remember just exactly how we were connected." Julia smiled wanly at Elizabeth.

"Well, no matter. 'Twas good fortune that we both had the measles while babies, for you would not have wished to miss this opportunity."

"Oh, Elizabeth, what if she does not like me?" Julia crushed the ribbons in her hand.

"Not like you! Don't be foolish. You are the most likable young lady of my acquaintance. Why, Lord Parks liked you even after you said his favorite horse looked touched in the wind."

Julia blushed even as she laughed. "I had no idea he was standing so close behind me when I said such."

"He must have valued your opinion, for he sold the animal as soon as he returned to Town."

The young ladies fell into conversation about mutual friends, and passed the next half-hour pleasantly. Elizabeth was glad to see she had distracted her friend, if only briefly.

Feeling the coach slow down for the turn into the gates at Langley Hall, Elizabeth gazed curiously out the window. As they passed through the stone pillars, the young ladies were afforded their first view of the estate.

Langley Hall was set in a large, rolling park on the

banks of the River Nidd. They couldn't see the waterway, but knew it lay beyond the house and out of view, having seen the map sent by Miss Langley. The prospect, clearly visible out the carriage window, was a long drive lined with neatly sculpted box trees which ran straight to a huge grey granite building. It had the impressive look of an ancient castle, but the workmanship showed it was clearly newer in years.

Elizabeth drew in her breath at the sight. "How beautiful. Look, Julia, the house has been built in the medieval style. One day we must inspect the turrets."

"Fancy someday bein' mistress of such a place, Miss Julia," Margie spoke up. She blushed when Elizabeth shook her head slightly to warn the girl not to bring up a subject which might add to her mistress's unease.

Julia's curiosity and interest overcame her nerves. " 'Tis far larger than Riverview. Mr. Ritter said the Hall is famous for its beautiful gardens."

"Mr. Ritter? When did you speak to the curate about Langley Hall?" Elizabeth looked at her friend, whose cheeks now flamed red. She saw her father's assistant nearly every day and did not know that he had spoken to Julia since she'd received the letter about the legacy.

"Well . . . that is . . . a-at the village inn on Wednesday."

"I see." Elizabeth suddenly wondered if the shy couple were meeting secretly. Mr. Jacob Ritter would not have been considered a suitable match by Lady Powers. Then, with a dismissive shake of her head, Elizabeth realized that Jacob was nearly as shy as Julia. The thought of a romance was unlikely, so she dismissed the matter from her mind.

At that moment the carriage pulled to a stop some thirty feet from the Hall. A footman exited one of the large oak-studded double doors that formed a Gothic arch at the top. He hurried up the long flagstone walk and over the bridged moat to assist the young ladies and the maid down, welcoming them to Langley.

"Oh, miss, 'tis like a fairy-tale castle with a moat and everythin'," Margie said.

" 'appens that there was put in by Mr. 'ubert Langley," the footman said. " 'E reckoned a 'ouse like this needed a moat. But don't be afeard. 'Tis only orna . . . er . . . ornamental and not very deep." The footman cast an appreciative glance on the pretty young maid, who giggled and blushed.

Following the talkative young servant in grey and wine livery to the house, they were greeted with severe formality by a white-haired butler, who announced, in ringing tones, that he was Aegis. Julia presented her companions before he escorted them into the Great Hall, a cavernous chamber with a beamed ceiling and oak-paneled walls, smelling of beeswax and turpentine.

The butler led them to an oak settle positioned before an oversized fireplace with an ornately carved overmantel. He offered refreshments, but the ladies declined. With his booming voice, he informed them that Miss Langley and her companion were at present resting and he would show the young ladies to their rooms, where they might do the same. Elizabeth suspected him of being slightly deaf, as his speech echoed eerily in the hall.

As the elderly man led them up the stairs, he hummed softly to himself. Elizabeth rolled her eyes as she looked at Julia who was just barely able to suppress a giggle.

They followed the butler down the main hall, past a line of doors, each with Gothic arches set in chamfered frames. At last the dignified servant ushered Julia into a large wainscoted room decorated with pale pink hangings. She meekly remained there after the butler informed her that she must rest and dinner was at seven.

After walking for what seemed a great distance, Aegis then settled Elizabeth in a bedchamber similar to Julia's, only done in green in the west wing. The old man left her alone in the large wood-paneled room. The sound of his loud voice echoed down the corridor as he questioned Margie about her journey while he led her to the servants' quarters.

Walking round the chamber as she removed her bonnet, Elizabeth admired the well-polished satinwood furnishings, the Belgian black marble fireplace, and the three tall windows with medieval depressed arches and diamond-cut quarries. Running her hand over the gleaming wainscoted oak wall, she wondered about the task of being mistress to such a large establishment, and was glad that the parsonage was far smaller.

A knock sounded on her door, and a young maid entered bearing hot water. "Good day, miss. I'm Annie and will take care of ye while ye stay at the 'all."

"Thank you, Annie. Do you think Miss Langley would mind if I took a walk in one of the gardens after I freshen up? I have been sitting in that carriage much of the day and could use some exercise."

"Why, no, miss. The gardens are Miss Langley's pride and joy. To be sure, ye must go see the Statue Walk what madam designed 'er ownself."

"That sounds interesting. How might I find this walk?"

"Go through the Rose Garden, then cross the moat, and there is the first statue of a little Greek girl. 'Tis quite lovely, miss."

Some fifteen minutes passed before Elizabeth finished freshening up and found a pair of sturdy walking shoes. At last, she ran a comb through her crushed curls, and finding a straw bonnet among the apparel the maid had unpacked, she set out to see if Julia wished to join her, but discovered that her friend had taken Aegis's advice and had lain down to rest.

With the help of a footman, Elizabeth made her way

to the Rose Garden, gleaning a bit information along the way. "Are we the first to arrive?"

"No, Miss Fields. A Miss Bradford and 'er mama arrived early this mornin', and Miss Shelton and 'er brother came near one o'clock. Your Miss Powers was the last we was expectin'."

"That is not such a large party." Elizabeth felt relief that there would only be four other relatives, though she wondered if all were being considered for the legacy.

"There is the Statue Walk, miss, just beyond the small bridge."

"Thank you."

The servant left Elizabeth to explore on her own. She strolled to the bridge, stopping to watch the goldfish swimming in the moat below. Fascinated with the colour and size of the fish, she decided to walk along the edge of the moat first. She ambled along the man-made waterway until she came to a spot under a large birch tree.

Settling herself in the shade at the water's edge, she removed her chip-straw bonnet and leaned over to stroke her fingers through the cool water. The small fish, frightened by the ripples on the surface, darted away, then slowly came back to see if they were to be fed.

The June afternoon was sultry. On a sudden impulse, Elizabeth looked around to see if she was observed, then removed her half boots and stockings to dangle her feet in the cool water. She felt lighthearted and unfettered by responsibilities. She hadn't done anything so unabandonedly foolish since assuming her mother's role in taking care of her brothers and sisters.

A warm breeze rustled the leaves above her, and she caught the sweet scent of honeysuckle. Elizabeth wondered how Miss Lilian was faring at Aylsham. Was Ruth spending too much time at the stables? Had Sarah gone out for any exercise, or had she buried her nose in a novel? Had John and Matthew arrived home? Elizabeth was certain that even if her sisters had not heeded her admonishments, no great harm would be done in so short a time as her visit would take.

Looking out over the beautifully landscaped park, she was certain that Julia could be happy in this gentle setting. In truth, if need were the measure by which Miss Langley was judging her relatives, her friend would surely qualify.

The late Lord Powers had left his estate near ruin, what with his gaming and poor investments. The girl was virtually dowerless, and Lady Powers felt what few funds she had must be saved for Edward and his needs. A cold woman, the baroness was often heard to blame her daughter for lacking sufficient address to attract a wealthy suitor.

Ironically, Lord Powers had been Julia's greatest defender against the barbs of her mother. When in residence, which was rare, he'd taught his daughter to tool his curricle and had taken her with him to hunt. Equally useless skills for a young lady in the baroness's opinion. With her father gone, Julia now suffered the full brunt of her mother's sharp tongue.

While Elizabeth sat lost in thought, a sudden gust of wind caught the straw bonnet she'd tossed to the ground. Before she could catch it, the hat landed on a cluster of hyacinths in the moat, its long blue ribbon trailing in the gentle flow of the water.

Elizabeth strained to reach the ribbon, but it was just beyond her outstretched fingertips. She got up on her knees, thinking she might grasp the bonnet from that position. Extending herself as far as she could, she barely touched one of the ribbons. She leaned out a tiny bit further.

"Madam, have a care!"

The unexpected voice startled Elizabeth so, she lost her balance and, with a soft scream, tumbled headfirst into the moat. The water was not unbearably cold, but she had no wish for the soaking she got.

She struggled to get her footing, but the bottom was slippery and she took another dunking for her efforts. She managed to grab the stone wall on the opposite side and steadied herself enough to plant her feet.

With water streaming over her eyes, Elizabeth looked about for the owner of the voice which had caused her to fall. About to utter a biting comment, the sarcastic words stuck in her throat when she found herself staring into the green eyes of a frowning soldier. His arm was extended as if he'd tried to catch her.

After a moment she noted a young girl standing behind him, her eyes rounded in shock and a pair of dainty hands over her mouth. The gentleman was the one who captured Elizabeth's attention, though, for he was the most handsome man she had ever seen. His raven black hair gleamed in the sunlight, and his emerald eyes stared at her from a sun-bronzed face.

Oh, dear, Elizabeth thought, how had this happened? She felt about the same age as Ruth. Here she stood, soaked to the skin, her hair dripping in her eyes, and, if she was not mistaken, fish swimming under her gown.

# Two

"Roderick, do jump in and save her," Imogene urged as she trailed behind her limping brother to the edge of the moat. As they came forward, the young lady struggled in the water, but within seconds the unfortunate miss found her footing. She surfaced, staring back at them with dazed eyes.

The major advanced as rapidly to the water as his wounded leg would allow, then realized the girl was safe when he saw her stand. He murmured to his sister, " 'Tis but a few feet deep, child. She merely needs assistance to be lifted out, and I can do that better from the bank."

He arched one dark eyebrow, uncertain what to say to the woman. She was surely a complete hoyden or a total provincial to have been sitting with her feet in the water. He eyed the faux water nymph closely.

At present, she was rather a bedraggled sight with her wet hair plastered to her face and hanging in long dripping tendrils about her shoulders. Her only noteworthy features were a pair of fine blue eyes and a full rosy mouth, which at the moment was agape. Surely, he reasoned, this ungraceful creature would be no competition for his vivacious sister in the contest for Miss Langley's legacy.

Addressing the lady, he inquired, "Are you unharmed, madam?"

The young woman was silent for a few moments, then lightly shook her head as if sorting her wits. "Only my dignity has sustained an injury, sir."

"I am Miss Imogene Shelton." The major's sister smiled eagerly down at Elizabeth. "This is my brother, Major Roderick Shelton. You must allow us to help you out at once, before you catch your death of cold, Miss . . ."

"Elizabeth Fields. I am very pleased to make your acquaintance, and I hope you will forgive my present state. I should never have removed my bonnet." Elizabeth didn't mention the removal of her shoes. Her hope was that the pair would not mention her unconventional behavior to Miss Langley, for that might harm Julia's chances. She lifted her straw hat which now ran with blue dye from the tiny artificial flowers that hung limply from the brim.

Imogene glanced at her brother who seemed to be sternly nodding his agreement. Remembering his preoccupation with the priorities, she felt a need to absolve the unfortunate miss from any pretext of wrongdoing. "*I* can see how one could not resist removing one's hat on such a lovely day, Miss Fields, for they can be so confining."

"You sound very much like my younger sister. I daresay she would find a great deal of amusement in my present situation."

The major, making no comment, reached down, offering the drenched miss his hands. He easily pulled her from the water, but was surprised to find a lady who stood only as tall as his chin. Perhaps more startling was that her dripping blue gown clung to a well-shaped feminine form.

Seemingly not the least bit embarrassed, Miss Fields dropped her ruined bonnet to the ground and began to shake out the layers of her skirts. "I believe I picked up a passenger."

A tiny fish dropped to the ground from underneath the cloth, flopping about desperately. While she continued to shake the fabric, the major, who'd stepped back to avoid being splashed, swept the small creature back into the moat with the toe of his Hessian.

"Oh, dear," Imogene cried. "Do you think it will suffer?"

"It's doubtful any harm shall come to it from such a short journey." The major's mind was busy trying to take the measure of this strange female. The task gave his face an intense look.

His first thought was that the young woman he'd pulled from the water was decidedly lacking in sensibilities. What genteel female would not be overwrought by falling into a moat, yet this chit behaved as if it were a daily occurrence as she stood conversing in her bare feet. But that reflection was quickly lost as he admired her barely concealed form.

Attempting to remove some of the water from her gown, Elizabeth eyed the brother and sister with interest, wondering which was to be considered Miss Langley's possible inheritor. She hoped Miss Shelton was the candidate, for the major was far too impressive in his regimental jacket. Even an older lady would find it difficult to ignore his appeal.

Roderick turned to his sister, forcing his eyes away from the enticing shape revealed by the wet gown. "Imogene, help Miss Fields to her room."

Elizabeth contradicted him as she unhanded her skirts. "Nonsense, sir. You and your sister should continue upon your walk. I shall enter through the kitchens, for I don't wish to leave a dripping mess in the Great Hall. I can find a maid to assist me on the way to my room."

Imogene saw her brother's brows draw inward at Miss Fields's refusal to follow his directions; then he turned to stare at the landscape as if what the lady did or didn't do was of no concern to him. She was certain he was quite used to being obeyed in all things. Suppressing a grin at his consternation, she said, "Oh, I don't mind accompanying you. My brother and I have plenty of time to explore the gardens. Why, you and I might discover if we are perchance related. You are come to Langley Hall about Cousin Esmé's legacy, are you not?"

"Not I, Miss Shelton. I merely came as friend and companion to Miss Julia Powers, who might be a relation to you and your brother." Elizabeth noted the major seemed to be avoiding looking at her as he kept his gaze locked on the well-manicured gardens beyond the moat. She was not surprised, for she was likely an untidy sight with her hair hanging in wet ringlets and her gown dripping water. She tried to pull the soaked material away from her body to keep from being too indecorous.

"Oh, Roderick is but my half brother. My connection to Miss Langley is through my mother. But I have promised him that if I inherit I shall invite him—"

"Imogene, do not delay Miss Fields from retiring to her rooms with your chattering. She will catch a chill if she stands here much longer." Roderick was amazed at how unguarded his sister was in her confidences with a complete stranger.

Eyeing the frown on the major's handsome face, Elizabeth was not certain if he disapproved of his sister's open manners or of herself for standing around and dripping like a tree in a rainstorm. "Sir, I am never sick, so do not worry on that account. But I would ask one favor."

Major Shelton stiffly bowed. "I am at your service, Miss Fields."

"Might I borrow your half-cape to cover my gown? I have heard that the ladies of London are known to dampen their underskirts before going out, but I don't believe soaking wet is the style." Elizabeth smiled at the major as he quickly released the thin cord which held the small decorative cape to the back of his uniform. He was obviously trying to impress Miss Langley, Elizabeth realized, for he was in his full military dress.

Settling the garment on her shoulders, Roderick stepped back when he caught the intoxicating scent of jasmine from her. In a stilted tone, he uttered, "I apologize for not thinking of offering it sooner, Miss Fields."

"Well, I thank you for it now, sir. Please continue your walk. I understand there is something called the Statue Walk just beyond the bridge." Elizabeth bid them good day, then bent down to retrieve her bonnet, shoes, and stockings. She gingerly started to the rear of the Hall, hoping nothing sharp lay in the grass to injure her unshod feet.

As she moved through the neatly trimmed shrubbery, her thoughts were on the pair she'd just met. She was sure she liked Miss Shelton with her easy manners and gentle smile, but of the major she was left in uncertainty. There was no denying that he was excessively handsome, but he'd seemed remote and disapproving during their brief encounter.

With a shrug of her shoulders, Elizabeth tried to dismiss the soldier from her mind. She must concentrate on helping Julia and not worry about Major Shelton.

Beside the moat, Imogene looked up at her brother curiously. She had come to know him well enough over the past few weeks to realize that in some way he was distracted. Had he been so scandalized by the young lady? "I do hope Miss Fields does not take cold from her fall."

Roderick offered his sister his arm, then led her back towards the bridge. "She said she is never ill."

"Do you not like her? I found her quite pleasant, and I don't know many of my friends who would have handled an accident so unaffectedly."

"The lady carried herself well enough." Roderick did not want to tell his sister that the miss in her wet gown had affected him in some strange way and far more powerfully than he wished. He knew the course he'd plotted for his future, and a woman was not any part of that plan.

Crossing over the stone bridge, he inquired, "Shall we find the Statue Walk?"

Miss Esmé Langley lay on a rose and gilt upholstered couch in her bedchamber, her eyes closed as she stroked the small, smooth-haired fox terrier beside her. A surprisingly girlish cap topped her snow white hair, and a fashionable gown of forest green encased her tall, trim body. At the age of sixty-five she still enjoyed dressing in the latest styles, despite the crippling effects of arthritis which required the use of a cane.

The long cold winter and a serious lung congestion, however, had left her with such a feeling of *ennui* that for the first time in her active life she had seriously contemplated what would become of her vast estates after she was gone. So, two months earlier, and with the help of her man of business, she'd formulated a plan. They had scoured her extended family tree for suitable young ladies to become the future Langley heiress.

Three worthy young girls had received invitations from Esmé with full explanations. Now, with the aspirants under her roof, she worried that she might have made a mistake, for few young ladies were educated for the task she had in mind.

Opening her eyes, she pondered whether she should have considered Sir Gordon Mondell, her closest male relative, but life often seemed unfair to Esmé in regard to females and their lot. She had it within her power to pass her estate to a female. Hopefully, she could find one who would use the fortune to the fullest extent for her own happiness. But the lady would also need to be able to handle the business side of the estate. Only time would tell her if one of the girls presently at the Hall might fill her stylish shoes.

"Oh, Reynard, I do hope that the young ladies I invited will enliven the Hall, so it will be as it was when I was young." She stroked the dog's brown and white spotted fur as he cocked his head intelligently, seeming to sympathize with his beloved mistress. "Whatever shall I do if there is not one among them who is strong enough or worthy enough to take on the responsibilities of being the Langley heiress?"

Reynard issued a soft bark as if in answer to her question.

A sharp knock sounded on the door, interrupting Esmé's thoughts. She bade her visitor to enter.

Miss Prudence Hartman, the heiress's companion for twelve years, swept into the room, a lace handkerchief clutched to her lips. Clearly the lady was distressed.

"Esmé, the most dreadful thing has occurred." Miss Hartman made a point of standing on the opposite side of the sofa from Reynard, for she had a strong dislike of the animal, which he in turn reciprocated. She was dressed in a high-necked black dress, still being in perpetual mourning for her father who'd died ten years earlier. The dark-hued gown gave the skin on her thin, angular face a pallid appearance. A large cap with black ribbons nearly obscured the greying hair which frizzed about her face.

"Now, Prudence, what has overset you? Have not all the young ladies arrived?" Esmé kept a hand on the small dog, who'd stood and growled in the most menacing manner.

"They are here, but . . ." Prudence edged back a step when the dog made another low growl in his throat. She kept a wary eye on him and continued. "But your solicitor was incorrect about Miss Shelton's half brother being with his unit in the Peninsula. He . . . is *here*. You said that

Miss Johnson or one of the other teachers would most likely accompany her from her school in Bath."

"Really, Prudence, is that what has you so nettled? Why, as to that, I have no problem with his accompanying his sister to Langley. I always did think a gentleman seated at dinner helps stimulate the conversation. I should like to hear what he thinks of that little Corsican devil."

In a voice filled with condescension Miss Hartman replied, "Oh, Esmé, you are such an innocent where gentlemen are concerned. You, who were sheltered your whole life by your papa, have no notion of what slaves men are to their lusts. I cannot think it safe to have three unmarried misses exposed to the major's carnality, for Miss Powers has a young woman of gentle birth accompanying her. We shall have a scandal if we do not do something."

Leaning her head back on the sofa, Esmé chuckled. Over the years she had never quite gotten the full story of the failed romance which so coloured Prudence's thoughts, giving her companion a distrust of all men, with the exception of the clergy. "Poor Major Shelton, are you not to give him the benefit at the doubt, dear Pru? He may prove to be perfectly harmless. Nothing in Mr. Jamison's investigation revealed anything out of order about the Shelton family. Except for some estrangement between the uncle and his brother's children, there is not a single blot to be found on the major's record."

Prudence sniffed indignantly. "I know nothing of reports. I can only give you the benefit of my experience, and you know how I was deceived by a *soldier* who stole kisses after promising to marry me."

"A soldier? You never mentioned the knave was a military man, but what would you have me do, my dear? I want to meet and assess Miss Shelton, so I cannot refuse to house her own dear brother."

"Why, send him to the Golden Pheasant in the village."

Prudence Hartman looked at Esmé as if it were the simplest thing to turn a guest from her door.

The aging heiress lifted Reynard as she slowly lowered her satin-slippered feet to the Aubusson carpet. Prudence backed towards the door as Esmé tried to reason with her. "Using what excuse? Not enough spare rooms in a house with thirty-five bedchambers? Don't be ridiculous, Prudence. If you are uncomfortable at having an unmarried young man in the house, I urge you to invite the Reverend Mr. Tyler to join us for dinner this evening. Not even the most hardened rake would misbehave before such a prosing paragon of virtue."

"An excellent suggestion. I shall send a message at once." Reynard barked and Miss Hartman made haste for the door, but was halted by her mistress's voice.

"Have all the arrangements for our guests entertainment been handled?"

The companion turned and nervously wrung her handkerchief as she watched Esmé's pet squirm to be put down. "I have taken care of everything. I was thinking a small ball would be nice as well, so that the young ladies might meet the families in the neighborhood."

Esmé, using an amber-topped cane, walked to the window. Looking out at the setting afternoon sun, she placed Reynard on the window seat as she turned to Prudence. "Perhaps, but I think I might do that at the end of the visit to announce my selection."

Seeing the small dog freed from his mistress's embrace, Miss Hartman squeaked, "I shall see to it." Then she quickly turned and fled the room.

Esmé scratched the dog's ear affectionately. "For such a small fellow, you do strike terror in that woman's heart, Rennie. You must strive to be nicer, old boy."

Reynard gave a quick bark and dashed across the room to the sofa to once again settle down as if the matter of Miss Hartman were of no importance to him at all.

* * *

Elizabeth sat by the window in the fading afternoon warmth, with a towel drying her newly washed hair. She found her mind kept going back to her encounter with Major Shelton. She remembered how the light played on his black hair as he'd frowned down at her. He was handsome even with his overly formal manner. She had heard that women were very susceptible to men in uniform. It must be true, she thought, for the first officer she'd encountered, outside of the sons of neighbors, intrigued her.

What good would it do to fancy herself in love, she sighed. She had a responsibility to help her father raise Ruth and Sarah. The boys were nearly grown, but she simply would not feel right abandoning the girls to Cook and a housemaid. They had lost their mother at such a tender age and for that Elizabeth felt a great deal of guilt.

Lady Powers's accusatory words to Elizabeth at the funeral of her mother would forever echo in her mind: *If you had not been such a trial to your mother, perhaps she would not have succumbed at such an early age.*

Deep in her heart, Elizabeth longed for the things other young women had—a home of her own, a husband, and a family. Destiny seemed to be telling her it was not to be, but could she make her heart obey?

A knock sounded, interrupting her thoughts, and she heard Julia call, "Elizabeth, are you awake?"

"Very much so."

Her friend entered the room, then halted. "I did not know you meant to wash your hair."

Elizabeth laughed. "I had not intended to, but a quick swim in the moat changed my mind."

"You went swimming in the moat!" Julia's tone was shocked. "Lizzie, I-I cannot think that Miss Langley would approve of such behavior. I know that you and Matthew used to sneak away to swim in the river behind the vicarage, but—"

"I was teasing, Julia. I fell in, and Major Shelton and his sister came along and pulled me out."

Julia, who had closed the door and come to sit beside her friend, eyed her curiously. "They are here about the inheritance as well?"

"Only Miss Shelton, for it seems that she and the major have only their father in common and the Langley connection is through her mother."

"I wonder how many others there are?" Julia gazed out at the gardens, a wistful expression on her face. She had been surprised at how much she liked her surroundings.

Elizabeth placed a hand on one of her friend's. "Don't worry. The footman who showed me the garden said there is only a mother and daughter besides Miss Shelton. That is not such a great number."

"True." Julia smiled tensely across at Elizabeth. "I-I am trying not to be nervous. After all, Cousin Esmé cannot eat me, and I can be no worse off than when I started. Besides, I know I shall have Aunt Lilian to protect me when mother finds out I was not the one chosen."

Elizabeth thought her friend sounded more as if she were trying to convince herself. "Miss Wade? I don't see her as being a valiant protector. She is the sweetest-natured lady but always so quiet and docile in Society or at home doing your mother's bidding."

"There are great depths to that lady that few have seen. I think she is best described by a line from Shakespeare. 'Courage mounteth with occasion.' She is at her best when her fortitude is tested or when she is protecting her family. I just wish I could say the same about me."

"Don't let your mother's thoughtless criticisms undermine your courage. You are good, kind, and an excellent companion. Just try and be yourself. Miss Langley cannot help but appreciate you as your friends do."

Julia looked down at her clenched hands, forcing them to relax. "You always know what to say to make me feel better about myself."

"That is because I like and admire you excessively. Even during my madcap youth, you never judged me as others did." Elizabeth leaned over and gave her friend a hug. "Now, what shall you wear to dinner? I think your blue silk with the white lace overdress makes you look very fine."

Julia's eyes brightened as the subject changed to clothes. "I was thinking my white silk with the pink ribbons, for it is only two years old and the ribbons are quite new."

The ladies spend the remainder of the afternoon discussing what each would wear and how they should dress their hair until Annie came to dress Elizabeth for dinner. As the maid pulled her hair up into curls and threaded a blue ribbon through them, Elizabeth wondered if the handsome major would be less disapproving about her now that she was clean and dry and in her finest gown.

Roderick paused in the Great Hall some way from the double doors which led into what they were informed was the Egyptian Drawing Room. He wanted to give his sister a final word of encouragement. "Imogene, I hope you are not anxious about the outcome. You know that no matter what happens here, I shall always gladly provide for you."

"Nervous? Not in the least. But I do wish we'd had the time to get at least one new gown, for I feel quite the child in this horrid thing Miss Johnson ordered." Imogene looked down at the unadorned grey muslin dress, frowning.

"You look a proper young lady, my dear." He was pleased with her appearance, but did think the gown

made her look a trifle young with its high ruffled collar
and drab colour. He mentally made a pledge to treat her
to several new gowns even should she not win the legacy.
He took her small hand in his to add one bit of advice.
"You must promise me to mind your tongue, for you are
too apt to chatter about matters best left private."

"But Miss Langley is family, and we have no dark secrets, do we?" Imogene's brow puckered.

"Now don't frown when a smile suits your lovely face
much better." Roderick watch his sister grin with delight
at the compliment. "That's better. I am not chastising
you, just giving you a word of caution, my dear. Secrets
or no . . . people are often curious about our estrangement from Lord Kirtland. Besides, we are not related to
everyone invited here. I much prefer that we keep our
personal affairs private." So saying, he led her to the
drawing-room doors.

As the footman intoned, "Miss Shelton, Major Shelton," Roderick led his sister forward and surveyed the
amazing apartment. The room's name did not merely de-
note a fashionably done Egyptian interior, but a chamber
which resembled a museum of artifacts from the Nile region. He promised himself a day of going through the
exhibits which hung from the walls and sat behind glass
in cabinets, but for now he must concentrate on the
room's living inhabitants.

Four women and a man were already in the room. He
immediately spotted Miss Langley, looking very regal in
a crimson gown with matching turban. A small brown
and white dog sat on her lap, eyeing the visitors warily.
Roderick scanned the party and was surprised, even a bit
disappointed, to discover that Miss Fields was not yet
among the gathered guests.

"Major, Miss Shelton, will you join us in a glass of
sherry while we await the others?" Esmé eyed the young

lady with approval. The girl's eyes were full of excitement, without the lest hint of nervousness. A very good sign.

As the major moved a chair for his sister to sit nearer to the group, Esmé added, "Allow me to present, my guests, Mrs. Bradford, Miss Bradford, the Reverend Mr. Tyler from our village church and, of course, my companion, Miss Hartman."

Roderick made a formal bow, saying all the correct things, then took the glass of sherry the footman offered before moving to a position behind Imogene. While Miss Langley asked his sister about her journey, he took the opportunity to more closely observe the other members of the group.

Mrs. Bradford was a matron of large girth dressed in a bright lemon-coloured silk gown. The lady's dark eyes were narrowed cunningly while they peered at his sister with open hostility, taking in every aspect of the girl. The woman was clearly determined to have her daughter inherit Miss Langley's fortune.

Roderick shifted his gaze to the girl sitting on the green damask sofa beside her mother. Miss Bradford was a pretty chit with rather vacant brown eyes and golden blond curls. The young lady was dressed in a daringly cut lavender gown covered with ribbons and ruffles which only served to emphasize her tendency to plumpness. He was glad his sister's own attire was more subdued, for while Miss Bradford's apparel was likely the height of fashion, it seemed inappropriate for one so young.

Myra Bradford showed little interest in the conversation of her mother as she sat eyeing the major. She suddenly opened her fan and began to flirt openly, fluttering her eyes up at the soldier in an absurd manner. She'd always admired military men, especially young and handsome ones. She was only called to attention when her mother spoke of Town.

"You reside in Bath year round, Miss Shelton?" Mrs.

Bradford asked. "La, I would live nowhere but London, for that is where all the amusements are. Myra moves only in the first circles of Society."

Esmé looked at the woman as if she'd announced she was Cleopatra. The Langley solicitor had gathered a thorough report on the Bradfords. They lived quietly on the fringes of Society. Finances and a lack of acquaintances had barred them from moving with the upper Ten Thousand. No doubt they had gone into debt to acquire the girl's fashionable wardrobe.

Myra, unaware that her cousin knew her true circumstances, began the speech she'd rehearsed with her mother. "True, but I was glad to forsake my social calendar to come, for I am vastly honoured to be at Langley Hall. There is nothing like a visit to the country after such an exciting Season. Even Mr. Brummell said that I was looking burned to the socket from all the late nights."

Esmé was certain the mother was behind this social climbing ruse. She wouldn't hold it against Myra, for very often daughters had little say in the plans of parents.

Imogene, looking greatly impressed with Miss Bradford's claimed acquaintance with the famous arbiter of fashion, naively asked, "I have heard of Mr. Brummell even in Bath. Is the gentleman nice?"

Mrs. Bradford laughed with a high whinny. Her second chin jiggled as she made an effort to suppress her mirth. "Nice, child? It is of no importance. He is friend to the Prince, therefore he does not have to worry about such things, for everyone knows they are made if the Beau condescends to have a conversation with them. I encourage Myra to be seen with him at every opportunity."

The Reverend Mr. Tyler looked Miss Bradford over and seemed to find something lacking. Tilting his head slightly upward as if he were speaking directly to God, he placed his hands palm-to-palm at his chin, and orated in a droning voice, "I fail to see why Society would grovel over such an idle man who thinks of nothing but the cut of his coat. He is said to have a wicked tongue. Be ever aware of a serpent among us."

"Serpent!" Miss Bradford's eyes grew round. "There is a serpent at Langley Hall? In the moat or the river? I hate the country, for it is full of nasty, smelly creatures."

"Myra, watch your tongue." The mother gave the daughter a speaking look.

Miss Hartman tittered, "Mr. Tyler was referring to the Serpent in the Garden of Eden, my dear."

Reynard growled at the sound of the companion's voice, then quieted when his mistress stroked his head. Miss Hartman's face took on a hunted look as she sidled closer to the vicar beside her.

That gentleman ignored the animal's interruption. "I refer to the Serpent as the temptation to do evil, child."

Not wanting the clergyman to dampen her guests' spirits, Esmé turned to Roderick. "Major, I understand you are just returned from the Peninsula."

"I have been back nearly six weeks, recovering from a wound." Roderick hoped Mr. Tyler would not be about the Hall for the entire visit, for he found the gentleman overly pious.

The clergyman seemed to take a sudden interest in the major, to that man's dismay. "Are you invalided out, sir, or do you intend to return to the war? England needs all her fighting men with that madman Bonaparte running about the continent. Cannot let a trifling wound keep you from the fray."

"I mean to return once I have my sister's affairs comfortably settled." Roderick, ignoring the gentleman's hectoring tone, placed a hand upon his sister's shoulder and received a smile from the young lady.

Esmé watched the silent interplay between brother and sister. She was pleased to see genuine affection between the pair who were reported much apart. "I do hope you intend to remain here for the duration of Miss Shelton's visit, for Prudence and I have made a great many plans to entertain you."

"I should be delighted to stay, Miss Langley. In truth, I am greatly intrigued by your fine collection." The major gestured towards the cabinets that lined the wall.

"You may have all the time you like to enjoy the bits and pieces my father and I collected on our various trips to Egypt."

Despite her determination to do as her brother bid her and remain quiet, Imogene's natural enthusiasm over-flowed. She moved to the edge of her seat. "Have you traveled a great deal, Miss Langley?"

"I hope you will call me Cousin Esmé. Yes, my dear, I have seen much of the world." The lady looked pensively into the glass of sherry she held, as if seeing visions of faraway places.

"I should love to travel," Imogene said. "I have had to be content with Roderick's letters, but he rarely tells me about the exciting places he visits, only that he is well."

The vicar frowned at Imogene. "Child, he is not on the Grand Tour, but fighting Frenchies. There can be little he could say that is fit for a delicately bred female."

Roderick rushed to his sister's defense. "I fear the fault is with my writing, sir, and not with Imogene's expecta-tions. I am often at a loss as to what my sister would find of interest, we have been so long parted."

Before anyone had the time to comment, the drawing-room door opened. The footman announced, "The Hon-ourable Miss Powers, Miss Fields."

Roderick glanced curiously over his shoulder. Two young women entered the room, one dressed in white and the other in blue. His gaze brushed Miss Powers, and he found her a passably handsome miss with a sweet smile.

He looked at Miss Fields and froze. The bedraggled water nymph from this afternoon was in fact a stunning beauty! The young lady, properly dressed and groomed, had a heart-shaped face to accent the lovely blue eyes and rosy mouth. Her hair, now dry, was a glossy, rich brown and was pulled up into a profusion of curls, a blue ribbon twined through them.

Suddenly Roderick felt like one of the statues in Miss Langley's garden, for his breath was taken away.

# *Three*

Elizabeth entwined her arm with Julia's as they advanced towards the waiting group who watched them with varying expressions of welcome. She felt a slight tremor of fear run through her friend, then a perceptible stiffening of the girl's back as they entered the Egyptian Drawing Room. Elizabeth was encouraged that Julia might overcome her shyness and would be able to bravely face the strangers.

The bright red of the major's tunic drew Elizabeth's gaze. He stood still, nearly motionless, staring at her with an arrested expression on his handsome face. She suspected he might not even recognize her, she'd looked so awful on coming soaking wet out of the moat.

Embarrassed at the memory, she drew her gaze away from the gentleman. At once she spied the fashionably attired Miss Langley. The lady's eyes held a welcoming twinkle even as she surveyed them curiously.

Esmé stroked Reynard and scrutinized the entering pair with interest. Miss Powers was rather plain until her face lit with a smile, or perhaps she appeared so next to her beautiful companion. Julia's friend was a beauty, no doubt, but Esmé was far more interested in her young cousin.

Introductions were made and chairs found for Elizabeth and Julia. Before they took their seats, however, Julia went to pet the dog her cousin held. She'd always had a way with animals that mystified Elizabeth.

"What is his name?" Julia asked, rubbing the fox terrier's small head.

"Reynard." Esmé watched as her pet's eyes closed at the sheer pleasure of the girl's gentle strokes.

"Do be careful, Miss Powers!" Miss Hartman squeaked, her eyes bulging at the anticipated danger.

Julia merely looked at the lady curiously as she returned to take a seat beside Elizabeth.

"Don't pay any heed to Prudence. She and Rennie have mutually decided to dislike one another." Esmé paused and looked around at her gathered relatives and guests. Everyone sat quietly, gazing at her, waiting for her lead. "Well, my dears, what think you of Langley Hall?"

Elizabeth was surprised when her friend shyly responded first. " 'Tis . . . 'tis an unusual building, Miss Langley. The exterior is clearly medieval in design, but the interior appears of a more recent period."

"Very astute, dear." Esmé was pleased with Julia's response, for it showed intelligence, a necessary quality for the one who would eventually run her estates. "The house was originally designed by Sir Christopher Wren's associate, Hawksmoor, during the time he was in Yorkshire to build Castle Howard in 1699. But I fear my great-great-grandmother had her own ideas. She took his plans and had them completely altered so that it is no longer listed as one of his works. She much preferred the look of an ancient castle, but with all the modern conveniences of her day on the inside. There are some interesting features about the house which I shall show you all during your visit."

Fascinated, Elizabeth inquired, "Are the turrets decorative, or do they lead somewhere?"

"Only decorative, I fear. I shall have Miss Hartman give you a tour of the house later in the visit, if you should like." Esmé looked around at the three young ladies she was considering as her heirs, well pleased with their rapt attention.

Mrs. Bradford shifted on the sofa, making the fragile furniture groan in protest. Hoping to draw attention back to her own daughter, she said, "Myra and I were admiring the lovely tapestries in each of our bedchambers. She has quite the artist's eye for lovely things."

"Yes, I believe they are Flemish." Myra shot a quick glance at her mother, who gave just the slightest nod of her head as if urging her daughter onward. "I do so love the arts. Why, Lord Byron is forever telling me I have the soul of a poet as well as the heart of a painter."

"Lord Byron?" Imogene's eyes sparkled. The young poet was all the rage since the release of *Childe Harold's Pilgrimage* in March.

Mr. Tyler, upon hearing the name of the newly celebrated bard, tilted back his head and intoned, "Society is rife with Serpents leading our young to waywardness."

Elizabeth fought back a smile at the rector's overly self-righteous manner. Mr. Tyler was one who saw evil all round him. She was glad her own father was not such a clergyman, for life would have been unbearable.

As Miss Langley changed the subject to the fine weather, Elizabeth took that opportunity to observe the distinctive room in which they sat. She wished her father were here to see the display, for he'd always been fascinated by the ancient Egyptian culture.

"Well, Miss Fields, I see you, too, are interested in my little exhibit," Esmé observed.

Bringing her gaze back to the heiress, Elizabeth could not contain her enthusiasm. "My father and I have done a great deal of reading on the Pharaohs. If you don't object, I would like to examine the artifacts more closely after we have dined."

"We have arranged for cards in the Yellow Saloon later,

but perhaps the major would accompany you back here since he has stated a similar wish." Esmé smiled at Major Shelton, thinking him a devilishly handsome fellow.

Miss Hartman gasped, then eyed the major through thinned lids. What could Esmé be about, encouraging the girl to fall into the major's clutches? Clearly her mistress had not heeded her warning.

Elizabeth's heart skipped a beat as Major Shelton uttered, "Your servant, Miss Fields."

"Dinner," roared the nearly deaf Aegis, who'd quietly entered the room.

A footman removed Reynard, then the major offered his arm to Miss Langley. The party trailed the heiress and the major, whose slight limp was barely noticeable at the slow pace set by Esmé. At last they came to a large dining room, on its beamed ceiling a craved frieze depicting angels.

Elizabeth found herself seated between Miss Hartman and the vicar. One did not converse with the old gentleman, one listened while he orated on the subject of good works. Strangely, Esmé's companion sat glowering at Major Shelton as he quietly spoke with Julia and Miss Bradford.

What had the officer done to Miss Hartman to engender so much dislike? Elizabeth found it hard to believe that even an aging spinster was not affected by the broad shoulders encased in the red jacket or the strength of character visible in his handsome face.

Periodically, Myra Bradford would lay a hand on his arm, saying, "Oh, Major, I must tell you . . ." Then she would drop the name of someone in Society that meant little to any of the gathered group.

Roderick looked up from his wine glass to see Miss Fields surveying him closely. When his gaze met hers, she smiled, then turned to answer a question from Mr. Tyler. The major could see her exquisite profile clearly. Could that much beauty be unspoiled? he wondered. Not in his experience.

Curiosity about the chit got the better of him. Turning to Miss Fields's friend, he asked, "In what part of England do you and your companion reside, Miss Powers?"

"Well . . . w-we are from Aylsham, sir. 'Tis a small village some ways north of Norwich in the Broads. The Powers Barony goes back to Charles the first."

"And Miss Fields is some poor relation employed by your family?" Roderick waved away the footman who was serving wine.

"Oh, no, sir. S-she is the daughter of the vicar at Aylsham and my oldest friend."

"A reverend's daughter? Is she like many of the offspring of the clergy, forever kicking up a lark?" Watching Miss Powers's eyes widen before she looked back to her plate, Roderick suspected he had stumbled upon the truth.

"That is . . . all past now that she has taken her late mother's place in raising her younger sisters. Why, Lizzie barely even rides these days, despite having the best seat in the county. I always believed it was Matthew who led her into the scrapes, not the other way round."

"Matthew?"

"Her oldest brother. H-He was sent down from Oxford once last year, and Lizzie had nothing to do with that." The young lady glared at him as if daring him to impugn her friend again.

At that moment, Miss Bradford drew Roderick's attention. She began to recite another boring tale of her triumphs in London, relieving him from making any comment. As the girl chattered, he smiled politely, but allowed his gaze to drift back to the beauty who sat across the table. Perhaps there was more to Miss Fields than just a pretty face, but clearly the episode at the moat showed her hoydenish tendencies lurked just below the surface.

What proper gentleman would be attracted to a young woman who would very likely spend her life in a scrape? Dozens and dozens, he thought as he took another look at her beautiful face, but not him. He had foolishly fallen prey to the wiles of another pretty chit. He had the memories of his former betrothed's defection to keep him from making the same mistake twice.

After dinner, the vicar took his leave, declaring he'd promised to drop in on Mrs. Stanley, a widow recently come to their village who needed his good counsel and advice. Except for Miss Hartman, none were sorry to see the last of the prosing gentleman.

While the card tables were being set up in the Yellow Saloon, Elizabeth found an opportunity to speak with Julia privately. "Whatever caused you to glare so at Major Shelton during dinner? I thought you were going to take your fan to him."

Julia looked over her shoulder to see the gentleman in question with his sister and Miss Bradford. The blond beauty appeared to be regaling them with some triumph from her Season as the words "Almack's and His Royal Highness" could be heard.

"Well, I was sorely tempted, but manners won out. He . . . he implied that you were something of a hoyden." Seeing her friend's raised eyebrows, she rushed on to continue. "I think it had to do more with the reputation that clergymen's children have garnered than your own actions."

Elizabeth laughed. "But I *was* something of a hoyden in my youth. No doubt he is judging me by our first meeting. In truth, I should not have had my feet in the moat this afternoon."

"Feet! I would say that much more than your feet entered the water."

Seeing Miss Hartman coming towards them, Elizabeth whispered, "True, but we should not speak of my accident in front of your cousin."

"Miss Powers, Miss Fields, do you play whist?" The companion eyed the pair eagerly.

"Julia is an excellent player, but I must beg off, for I have not the patience for cards."

"Then you, Miss Powers, must partner Esmé, for she does so love to win. I shall engage Mrs. Bradford in a game of piquet while the young ladies play whist with their cousin."

As Julia moved towards the tables, Miss Hartman placed a hand on Elizabeth's arm to detain her. "My dear, I know that Esmé suggested you and the major might tour the Egyptian artifacts while we play, but do you think it wise to do so alone with a strange gentleman?"

"Strange? Is there something you know about Major Shelton of which we should be informed?" Elizabeth felt an uneasiness at the thought of the soldier having an unsavory reputation.

Prudence became flustered. "Oh, dear me, I did not mean to imply . . . that is . . . Esmé will be angry with me. I should have said, unknown gentleman. I had an unfortunate experience with a soldier, and I try to warn young ladies not to be overly impressed with all that military bearing."

Suspecting the older woman viewed all soldiers as wicked due to her ordeal, Elizabeth struggled not to laugh. "I promise I shall keep my wits about me, Miss Hartman."

"I only meant that soldiers are very often fast. I suppose it comes from never knowing when one might die in battle. They look for their pleasures where they might find them." Miss Hartman hid her mouth behind her handkerchief as she whispered, all the while watching the major with hawklike eyes.

"I daresay that explains it." Elizabeth nearly laughed out loud. Esmé's companion was too absurd, for the major appeared anything but too coming.

Prudence, seeing Miss Fields could not be dissuaded, hurried to the tables to assist Esmé. She called to Miss Bradford and Miss Shelton to join Julia and Miss Langley, who were already seated across from one another at the table.

Elizabeth felt a flutter in her stomach as the major turned and came to her. He gave a slight bow, then, standing ramrod straight, stiffly inquired, "Shall we adjourn to the Egyptian Room for our tour, Miss Fields?"

She wasn't certain if he was so distant with everyone or just with ladies who fell in moats with their feet bare. "Please don't feel obligated to go with me, Major. I am quite capable of going alone. I am used to taking care of myself."

The major gave her an intense look. "I have no doubt you are a very able young lady, Miss Fields. But won't you allow me to join you, for I am equally interested in viewing the artifacts?"

Elizabeth was curious as to whether his experiences in the war had made him so serious, and she decided she would question Miss Shelton about her brother later. She found herself oddly fascinated with the gentleman.

Nodding her head in assent, she now permitted him to usher her out of the Yellow Saloon. As they walked down the stairs in silence, some of her old devilish sense of humor came to the surface. "So, Major Shelton, do you have a campaign strategy?"

Roderick looked a question at the beautiful young lady. A certain twinkle in her eye alerted him that he was about to be roasted. "Strategy about what, Miss Fields?"

"About winning the legacy for your sister. 'Tis plain to me that Mrs. Bradford has arrived with a well-laid plan. I think we are now aware that her daughter claims acquaintance with every fashionable member of the *ton.* Have you no such plan to promote your sister?"

The major gave her a half-smile. "And if I had such a plan, do you think it would be wise to reveal its nature to you?"

"I see you fear Julia might try and steal such a scheme, but that is not likely." Elizabeth tilted her head up to look at him. "She is too honest to attempt to promote herself on qualities or acquaintances she does not possess."

As they reached the foot of the stairs in the Great Hall, a footman moved to open the door to the Egyptian Drawing Room. Major Shelton allowed Elizabeth to enter the chamber first. As he paused to look around, he teased, " 'Tis early days in our visit. I might yet hear Miss Powers dropping famous names into her conversations."

"I doubt Miss Langley would be impressed if Julia were to tell her cousin that Dapper Darby thought her able to drive a curricle to an inch. He is one of the few notable residents living in our quiet village. While in Aylsham, Darby's opinion would be high praise, to Miss Langley it would mean little."

"True, for I don't believe any person of that name is being canonized in Society at present. How did he acquire such a title?" A smile lightened the major's features.

"He always wears a bright red cape with large green buttons and matching green hat . . . and very often his nose matches his cape."

At the description, Roderick's brows rose. "How remiss of the *ton* not to remember such a remarkable character."

Going to a cabinet full of small painted figures which appeared half-human and half-animal, the pair continued their light banter.

"The Polite World must be such slowtops, for he drove the London to Edinburgh stage for thirty years before a fondness for ale forced him to retire. He is quite famous at The Brown Duck."

Roderick was amused by the girl as he looked down into her twinkling blue eyes. She might be a hoyden, but she did have a great deal of charm. "If such a fellow praised Miss Powers's abilities, there can be little doubt of her skill with a whip. However, I must disappoint you, for I have no campaign for winning Miss Langley's fortune. I foolishly thought that the lady might like Imogene for her own merits."

"Then you do not think we should suggest, say a carriage race, or quizzing them on their knowledge of steam engines or poultices for sprained fetlocks to see which young lady is most capable of being the Langley heiress?" Elizabeth teased.

Unable to resist, Roderick laughed out loud. "No doubt a working knowledge of all those subjects is very high on Miss Langley's list of things an heiress must do and know, but I suggest we leave the matter in her hands. Shall we begin our inspection of this interesting room, Miss Fields?"

Elizabeth was surprised at how much she liked the sound of the major's laughter. "I should be delighted."

The yellow high-perched phaeton wheeled to a stop in front of Langley Hall. A foppish gentleman in a black beaver hat and ten-tiered driving cape jumped down to the gravel. In the silver moonlight, one could see he was of medium height and willowy build as he looked up at the brightly lit windows with a jaundiced eye.

As soon as the tiger grasped the reins, a second man in the sedate black of a servant joined the first. He lifted a bag from under the seat, before ordering the lad to the stables. Clutching Sir Gordon Mondell's heavy satchel, the valet leaned towards the baronet, his tone perfectly servile as he asked, "Sir, don't you think we should put up at the Golden Pheasant for the night? I can't think your cousin will be pleased, what with you interruptin' her party."

"Upon my soul, Ryland, this is a desperate situation. I shall not stand by and allow a bunch of tallow-faced chits to steal *my* inheritance." Sir Gordon advanced to the house, his Clarence blue cape billowing out as he walked, revealing the yellow satin lining.

Ryland knew he had as much at stake here as his master. Years of living in cramped rooms off St. James Street and putting up with the baronet's excesses were to be rewarded by the acquisition of vast wealth when Sir Gordon's cousin stuck her spoon in the wall. But the letter from the upstairs maid he'd wisely befriended on past visits had sent a shock wave through their world.

The Old Cat was going to leave her fortune and estates to one of her female relatives! It was not to be borne.

Following behind his master over the small bridge that led to the front door, Ryland shifted the heavy portmanteau that he had hurriedly packed to his other hand. "Have you a plan, sir?"

Mondell stopped, turning to his man and conspirator. "Yes, and I shall need your help. You must find out all you can about these pushing creatures from the servants' gossip. Any little tidbits I might be able to drop in my cousin's ear to give her a distaste for them."

"And if that don't work?"

"Then I shall think of some other scheme, for I have spent too many years dancing attendance on Cousin Esmé to be done out of that fortune. Losing those funds don't bear thinking about." Sir Gordon yanked off his hat in frustration, revealing golden blond hair crimped into neat curls about an Adonis-like countenance.

"Perhaps I might make a suggestion." Ryland had been struck by a plan as soon as he'd read the letter. It was not a concept that was likely to please the young dandy. "If all else fails, you might consider gettin' leg-shackled to the lady that is chosen."

"Marry one of these grasping harpies? You know my heart belongs to Lady Jane Bigelow." Sir Gordon sighed as a vision of loveliness flashed in his mind.

The valet bit his tongue to keep from shouting at his master. This was no time for the fop's foolish affectations. Instead Ryland calmly noted, "You know her father's in Dun Territory and she must recoup the family fortune by marriage. Should you lose the Langley legacy, then you lose the lady as well."

Sir Gordon kicked a large stone which lay among the gravel. "I shall first try to discredit these fortune hunt-resses. Then if that does not work, I might consider other options."

So saying the young man walked up to the door and lifted the knocker, hitting it hard against the door three times as if he were doing in the unwanted young ladies inside.

Elizabeth accepted the cup of tea Miss Langley offered her; then she moved to sit beside Julia. Her visit to the Egyptian Room had been cut short when Miss Hartman arrived in the chamber to say they must return for tea. The companion had seemed almost disappointed not to find the major mauling Elizabeth.

Taking a sip of tea, Esmé looked at the two on her right. "I wish to take you about the estate tomorrow. Do you and Miss Fields ride, my dear?"

Julia looked up nervously as all eyes seemed to be upon her. "There . . . there is little else to do in Aylsham. We often ride whenever Elizabeth is not engaged. I must ad-mit, however, that she is by far the more intrepid rider."

Elizabeth felt the major's gaze on her as she rushed to

defend her friend's reputation. "Don't let Julia cozen you, Miss Langley. She is equally dauntless, but in a different style. Her father trained her to handle the ribbons as good as any gentleman. I feel safer with her than with my own brothers."

Mrs. Bradford, who'd just taken a large bite from a poppyseed cake, shook her finger at Julia while she chewed. "Women should not be driving carriages. Why, much of Society has given Letty Lade the direct cut due to her antics. 'Tis too fast by far."

Roderick noted a crushed look appear in Miss Powers's eyes at the cruel comment, and Miss Fields's lovely face flushed angrily. Uncertain why, he intervened. "A lady might drive without harm to her reputation, Mrs. Bradford. I believe that the dauntless Letty's failing is bringing attention to herself by racing her carriage."

Imogene Shelton, who'd been surprisingly quiet much of the evening spoke dreamily. "I do so love a pretty carriage. I cannot resist the sight of a gentleman . . ." The girl's voice trailed off as she realized what she'd said. She bit her lip and shot a penitent glance at her brother.

Esmé set her cup on the table, watching the verbal sparring with amusement. "Julia, since I can no longer sit a horse, would you be kind enough to drive me out tomorrow?"

Julia blushed. "I-I should be honoured."

Mrs. Bradford's eyes narrowed as she glared at Julia, then she said, "You do want Myra and Miss Shelton to go as well, do you not?"

Esmé smiled. "Everyone must go. I insist."

At that moment, the drawing-room door opened and Aegis bellowed, "Sir Gordon Mondell."

A silence fell in the room as a veritable Bond Street Beau entered the chamber with a flourish. His impact was great on the room of unmarried young ladies. Blond curls glistened in the candlelight as he stood, posed, inside the doorway. He wore a striped garnet coat over a black and garnet checked waistcoat with pale grey pantaloons. But the most noteworthy feature of the gentleman was his face. His features bore a strong resemblance to those of a sculpted Greek God.

Raising his quizzing glass, he boredly inspected the occupants before sauntering forward to his cousin. "Upon my soul, Cousin Esmé, I appear to have interrupted a party."

The heiress smiled at the baronet, wondering how he had gotten word about her plans. She'd suspected his random visits were for no other purpose than to entice her into leaving him her fortune. No doubt he was here to cause mischief. With a chuckle, Esmé decided it didn't matter, for he would merely add to the fun. "Welcome to Langley Hall, Sir Gordon. I am vastly amused to see you here."

# Four

Elizabeth rose early the next morning as was her usual habit at Aylsham. She'd already donned a white muslin gown with green dots and matching ribbons when Annie arrived with hot chocolate.

"You should've rung, miss," the servant urged, coming into the room.

"I was sure you must have morning duties that I did not wish to interrupt. Besides, I am used to taking care of myself." When the maid's eyes grew wide at such a statement, Elizabeth quickly added, "But I would welcome help with my hair." She took a seat in front of the satinwood dressing table.

The servant began to brush out Elizabeth's long brown curls. "There aren't many of the guests up as yet, miss. But I believe Miss Langley and Sir Gordon will be in the breakfast parlour if ye 'urry, for I passed the gentleman in the 'all just now and my mistress never stays abed past seven in the mornin'."

"I would not have expected a fashionable gentleman like the baronet to rise so early in the country."

"Well, I think 'e's tryin' to flummery 'is way back into bein' Miss Langley's 'eir, not that 'e ever was, if ye want my opinion."

Elizabeth was curious about the baronet. He was clearly

an unexpected guest, but their hostess had welcomed him gladly. "Does Sir Gordon visit Langley Hall often?"

Annie's face puckered into a frown as she tried to work with one stubborn curl. "Two or three times a year, 'im and that sneaksby 'e calls 'is valet arrives uninvited. But Miss Langley does like to entertain. She's not likely to turn someone from the door."

Elizabeth's brows rose as she watched the girl in the mirror. "You don't like Sir Gordon's man?"

"Ryland's the type what listens at doors. 'E's always been a little too interested in what's 'appenin' at Langley durin' their absence. Took to courtin' Trudie ever' time 'e comes, but I think it's because she's got a tongue what runs on wheels."

Suspecting that the pretty young maid's nose might be out of joint because she wasn't the one the valet chose to set up a flirt with, Elizabeth made no comment.

Annie, not in the least fazed by the lady's lack of response, continued with her tale. "I don't know if I should be tellin' ye this, but Ryland is askin' all kinds of questions about the young ladies Miss Langley invited. Been trailin' after Miss Powers's maid and the major's man like a bird 'untin' a worm." The servant gave a deep chuckle. "But Aegis dropped a word in their ears and they're not givin' 'im the time of day."

Elizabeth smiled, wondering if the pair could still hear if the butler whispered as loudly as he spoke. She knew she shouldn't be listening to servants' gossip, but she instinctively felt that Sir Gordon Mondell intended no good by his unexpected arrival at Langley Hall. She was curious as to what the valet expected to learn. Most likely he was a spy for the baronet, for surely what profited Sir Gordon profited Ryland.

When the maid finished her hair, Elizabeth thanked the girl and sent her about her business. She remained at the dressing table, pondering the information the young servant had just dropped. She would have to keep a close eye on Sir Gordon. He appeared to be using his valet to play some deep game.

She wanted Julia to be Miss Langley's choice, but Elizabeth would engage in no deceit to help her friend. Neither would she tolerate any treachery by someone bent on furthering another's cause.

On that thought, Elizabeth made her way to Julia's room. Her friend was not out of bed, but she promised to be down as soon as she was dressed and sent Elizabeth on to the breakfast parlour.

As Annie predicted, Miss Langley and Sir Gordon were already seated in the oak wainscoted room, which looked the colour of honey in the sunlight. The gentleman wore a pale green coat with a green- and white-striped waistcoat and white pantaloons. The heiress looked like a somber shadow in brown silk as she sat beside the fop.

Surprisingly, Reynard was present as well. The dog sat beside his mistress on a cushion in a gilt chair and dined in style. He exhibited perfect table manners and waited patiently for any little treat that might be offered.

"Good morning, my dear," Esmé called. "Sir Gordon, you remember Miss Fields from last evening."

"I believe she is companion to one of your guests." The gentleman rose and swept a disinterested glance her way. "Your servant, miss."

Elizabeth quickly took a seat as the footman on duty served her. She inquired after the other members of the house party.

"You and Sir Gordon are the only ones stirring besides Prudence and myself." Esmé gestured to the trio of windows behind her, from which Miss Hartman, in oversized bonnet, could be seen cutting roses in the small garden that lay inside the perimeter of the moat.

The companion, glancing towards the Hall and seeing

herself being observed, gave a brief wave. Then she picked up her basket and moved to the next bush.

"Do you always rise so early, my dear?" Esmé thought the girl was exceptionally pretty and wondered at her still being unmarried. It was curious that Sir Gordon was not the least swayed by her beauty.

"We don't have many late nights at the vicarage. I find I get much more accomplished before the rest of the family rises." Elizabeth looked across at Sir Gordon. His mouth was set in a petulant line. She could see he was unhappy to have his private conversation with his cousin interrupted.

Esmé nodded, then took a piece of bacon from her plate and fed Reynard. "Do you ride with us this morning, my dear? I have arranged mounts for you with Squire Graceson. He is famous for his racing cattle and has produced three winners at Newmarket in the last ten years."

"I should be delighted. Do you join us, Sir Gordon?" Elizabeth asked the gentleman as he toyed with the food remaining on his plate. She thought it might be wise to keep herself aware of his movements.

Sir Gordon ignored her, instead turning to his relative. His tone was a mixture of gallantry and disparagement. "May I offer my carriage to you, cousin, if you intend to go with these . . . ladies?"

Esmé's eyes twinkled. "Thank you, no. Miss Powers shall tool me about in my old curricle."

"That timid little mouse from last night—in the unfashionable white frock?" The baronet allowed his slender white hand to drop to the table as if the thought took his strength away. "Surely, you cannot mean to be driven by someone of whose skills you have no knowledge."

Elizabeth's fingers tightened on her fork. She resisted the urge to stick the utensil into the top of the fribble's hand. "I assured Miss Langley that Julia is a credible whip. Your cousin will come to no harm."

Sir Gordon raised his quizzing glass to stare at the young woman before him. Dismissing her as of no concern to his plan, he allowed the glass to drop. In a bored voice, he droned, "One sees so many cow-handed drivers on the roads, 'tis shocking."

Elizabeth pasted a patently false smile on her face. "No doubt, sir, *you* would know more about cow-handed driving than I, but Julia's father was a member of the Four-in-Hand Club. I think we need not fear for Miss Langley's safety."

Esmé chuckled, as Sir Gordon's haughty gaze settled on Elizabeth. Looking as if he were about to give her a stunning set-down, he remained silent, for Major Shelton entered the room.

Roderick noted the flushed cheeks of Miss Fields and the slight twitching of Sir Gordon's jaw. It took only a few moments to determine that pair had been exchanging barbs across the table.

Thinking he might ease the situation, he addressed his sister's cousin. "Good morning, Miss Langley, I hope you have no objection to my joining your ride this fine morning? I have brought my own mount."

"Good morning, sir, no objections at all. The more the merrier, Major. I have set the time for ten to allow everyone to make the ride."

Reynard barked, then jumped down and ran to the oak door. He turned to look at his mistress.

"Henry," Esmé called to the footman on duty. "Take Rennie for his morning walk."

The servant, dressed in grey and wine livery, quickly picked up the small dog and exited the room. In a matter of minutes a new footman entered the parlor to stand duty.

Sir Gordon gave Elizabeth one last spiteful glance, then

turned to his cousin. "Reynard is looking very fit. He is such a delightful little creature."

"I thought you threatened to have him roasted the last time you were here, when he scratched one of your new boots?" Esmé's mouth twitched as she watched her relative squirm.

"Well . . . that is . . . I was but teasing, cousin. I have a great fondness for animals." The baronet suddenly had an interest in the pattern on the Belgium linen cloth.

Taking pity on Sir Gordon's discomfiture, Esmé asked the major about his journey from Portugal. Conversation became rather general, with everyone being extremely polite.

At last Esmé rose with the aid of Sir Gordon, who'd jumped to his feet as soon as she stirred. "Now, I must leave you to finish your meal, for I am meeting with my bailiff. The others should be here soon, so do not worry about the propriety, Miss Fields."

"Allow me to escort you, Cousin Esmé. We did not get a chance to finish our private conversation." The baronet shot Elizabeth a look of dislike. He clung to his relative like ivy as she exited the room.

Elizabeth's face relaxed into a half-smile. "I am glad you arrived when you did, sir, for I was in great need of reinforcement."

"How brave of you to cross swords with Sir Gordon so early in the morning, Miss Fields." Roderick eyed the young woman over the top of his coffee cup. He marveled again at what a remarkably pretty woman she was.

"Crossing swords? No, I was trying to keep that gentleman from sticking one into Julia's back and her not here to defend herself. You would be well advised to keep Sir Gordon in sight at all times, for I think he is here to undermine Miss Langley's plans and grab the estate for himself by any underhanded means at his disposal."

"The legacy is hers to do with—what *is* Miss Hartman

doing?" His attention was drawn to the woman in the garden.

Elizabeth turned to see Esmé's companion peering at them through a large rosebush. She waved to Prudence in the garden. "The lady is making certain that you keep your mind on your breakfast."

Miss Hartman closed the parted limbs in the bush when she realized she'd been spied. Then she peeked around one side. Seeing that she was still being observed, she made a great show of cutting roses, all the while keeping her eyes on the pair in the parlor.

The major frowned as he watched the antics of the older woman. "What else would I come to the breakfast parlor for?"

"How lowering to think you care more for buttered eggs and ham than about debauching young females. What will Miss Hartman think of military men after your poor showing?"

A look of surprise crossed Roderick's face when her meaning took; then he threw back his head and laughed. "It astounds me what she seems to conclude. Is it me or all men in general she accounts lecherous cads?"

"Only soldiers, sir. I believe her heart was broken by a military gentleman."

Looking back out at Esmé's companion, Roderick shook his head in disbelief. The lady, having removed all the roses from the bush, still continued to savage the plant with her shears as she covertly watched them. "I think she will trim that rosebush to the ground if she keeps at the stems in that manner."

"You would not begrudge her this little bit of excitement surely. She probably lives an otherwise dull life." Elizabeth glanced back at the soldier, who was a striking figure in a plain maroon riding coat and black buckskins. She had a difficult time removing her gaze from his broad shoulders.

The major looked down at his plate, a frown slightly marring his countenance. "I believe that the quest for excitement is vastly overrated, Miss Fields. I have tried to convince Imogene of its dangers."

Elizabeth lifted her chin defiantly. "Like most gentlemen, I am sure you have gotten your fill of it, sir. We ladies rarely get to feel the exhilaration—"

The sound of barking, followed by high-pitched squeals interrupted Elizabeth. Looking out the window, she caught the comical sight of Miss Hartman dashing around the butchered rosebush in circles, Reynard yapping at her heels in hot pursuit.

"We must do something," Elizabeth commented, but the major had already started towards the large windows.

Roderick turned the latch and threw open the portal. He gave a shrill whistle. Both Reynard and Miss Hartman stopped. The companion tried to catch her breath, clutching her chest as she eyed her archenemy.

Elizabeth appeared at the major's side. "Here, I believe he might be enticed with this."

Roderick took the slice of bacon she offered. In a voice that brooked no refusal, he called, "Come, Reynard."

The small fox terrier stood stock-still, clearly torn. He looked first at the major and the possibility of some treat, then back at the object of his chase.

Finally, the small dog dashed toward the open window and, with a great running leap, jumped into Major Shelton's arms. Without the least remorse for his previous actions in the garden, he began to devour the offered treat.

Roderick turned to Elizabeth while the animal savored the bacon. "You might want to see to Miss Hartman. I believe she has had more excitement than a lady can handle for one day."

"Too true," Elizabeth agreed with a smile as she left Major Shelton with Reynard.

* * *

Some two hours later, after having sufficiently soothed Miss Hartman's nerves with tea and commiseration, Elizabeth changed into her riding habit. She crossed over the small moat and joined those at the stables who intended to ride. A feeling of delight rushed through her as she spied three sleek mares standing in wait for their riders.

Squire Graceson, the owner of the animals, was a large man, not given to airs. Dressed in a superfine brown coat and buckskins spattered with mud, he had a likable round face. He eyed the two gentlemen and four ladies with interest. "By George, Esmé, you are the only person I know that'd invite the scavengers in to pick the bones before the big event."

"Don't be silly, Squire. I cannot leave my fortune to a completely unknown person. Do you not think I have a delightful set of relatives?" Esmé sat in her curricle with Julia holding the ribbons and Reynard perched on the seat between them.

The squire scanned the group, then leaned close to the carriage. "Take my advice, leave your blunt to one of these fine gentlemen. Gels weren't trained for the task of financial management and are likely to squander it on clothes, jewels, or worse, some fortune hunter. Shouldn't allow the land to go to rack and ruin for want of a good man."

"And we don't know any gentlemen whose penchant for high living has done far worse to his estates," Esmé snapped, her eyes briefly resting on Sir Gordon, who stood pulling on a pair of lemon-hued riding gloves. She suspected he rarely visited his small estate and such inattention to the property was responsible for many of his current financial woes.

Graceson removed his battered beaver hat, scratching his bald head. "I guess there ain't no guarantee when it comes to picking an heir. Just thank the stars that you weren't saddled with a son who's a loose screw, chasing every bit of muslin to pass by."

Esmé knew the squire was referring to his own off-spring, who'd shagged off to Town as soon as possible, dissipating the fortune his late mother left him at every opportunity. "The boy is young and will likely outgrow his excesses."

The squire merely grunted. Then he turned his attention to the subject dearest to his heart. "I brought the best of the lot from my barns, the ones that weren't breeding or in training. Two of the mares are very gentle, but the grey is best with someone who has a firm hand. Didn't know there was to be gentlemen or I would have brought a couple of stallions."

Esmé waved her gloved hand in dismissal. "No need, the major and my cousin have their own mounts."

She inspected the gentlemen's horses with the eye of an accomplished rider. Major Shelton rode a quiet, well-ribbed chestnut while Sir Gordon had a showy bay which nervously shifted back and forth as the groom held the rein.

"Shall we set forth?" Esmé eyed the company. "Don't think it necessary to stay with Julia and I. If you should like to have a good run, feel free."

The three young ladies who were to ride came forward to make their choices after the squire told them the animals' names and abilities. Miss Bradford, looking dashing in crimson, seemed reluctant to choose. She simpered and begged the major's help in selecting a suitable mount, then went against his advice and chose the white mare to complement her outfit.

While Miss Bradford kept the major in conversation, Miss Shelton questioned Sir Gordon about his sleek carriage which she'd seen in the carriage house. Then she took the sweet-tempered roan her brother recommended.

She sat on her mount, eyeing Miss Powers in the curricle
with envy. A thought came to Imogene, perhaps she
might convince Roderick to give her lessons. A smile
touched her pretty face as visions of her driving a phaeton
flashed in her mind.

Elizabeth made her own selection. After settling herself
on the back of the dappled grey that the owner informed
her was called Luna, she arranged her blue skirts and
pulled the low-crowned black beaver more firmly over her
brown curls. A tremor of delight to be riding again swept
over her. She took her reins and impatiently waited for
the ride to begin.

Squire Graceson, after seeing everyone mounted, bid
the company good day, urging Esmé to keep his horses
as long as she was entertaining. He rode off in the opposite direction from the Langley party across the open
park.

Roderick found Miss Bradford had maneuvered her
horse to his side. She tried to draw his interest with a steady
stream of banalities which always seemed to be filled with
"I" and "me," but he quickly excused himself, saying his
horse was rather too spirited this morning to ride abreast.

After the lady nervously eyed his animal, she dropped
back to ride beside the carriage. Unfettered with a companion, he watched his sister closely as the group passed
through the gates at Langley. Having paid extra for Imogene to continue to ride at the seminary, he was pleased
to see she managed quite well with Graceson's sleek little
mare. He was concerned, however, to see her draw the
animal next to Sir Gordon's showy bay and begin chattering away.

If Miss Fields was right about that gentleman, he might
use something the artless child innocently let slip to do
her an injury. He would watch the dandy closely.

Thinking of the lady who'd given him the warning, he
allowed his gaze to move to Miss Fields's trim blue-clad

figure riding on the far side of his sister. She seemed to offer nothing to the conversation between Mondell and Imogene, but clearly listened with interest.

The lady handled the frisky grey with ease despite the horse's pent-up energy. She glanced back over her shoulder at him with a warm smile which made her blue eyes sparkle as the white scarf tied to her hat trailed in the breeze behind her. He tamped down a sudden urge to taste her pink lips.

Angry with himself, he gently spurred Orion forward, forcing his way between his sister and Mondell.

"Genie, shall we see what your horse is up to?" He ignored the baronet.

"I should like that." Imogene's green eyes lit with obvious delight at the invitation. "Do you wish to join us, Elizabeth?" she asked her companion, unaware that the lady was what her brother was trying to escape.

"I would love a good go." Elizabeth noted the frown on Major Shelton's face just before she urged her horse into a canter. She gave little thought to the matter as they picked up speed and the exhilaration of the ride took over. She urged her fleet mare into a gallop, following the rutted road as it wound its way between two stone fences toward a wooded grove. She could hear the hoofbeats of horses behind her, then only the sounds of the major's chestnut cantering alongside.

Turning to the gentleman, she called, "Miss Langley said we might have a good run. What say you?"

With a nod of his head, Roderick gently kicked Orion into a full gallop. He was surprised that Miss Fields was able to keep her mount alongside his. The squire clearly bred a remarkably fast animal.

The path they charged along entered the woods, then took a sharp turn to the right. As they thundered round the curve, Roderick was appalled to see a hay cart, one wheel tumbled to the ground, blocking their path. A young lad frantically waved his arms in warning.

The major instinctively reached for Miss Fields's rein, but the lady spurred her horse faster and sailed the animal over the stone fencing on her right.

That momentary attempt to aid the girl cost Roderick his speed. He tried to spur Orion forward to take the fence on the left, but the horse, eyeing the hay cart, came to a sudden grinding halt, sending the major straight over his head into the stack of hay.

Roderick felt no pain, only grinding shock and humiliation. He hadn't been thrown from a horse since he was seven years old. Somehow in the rush of emotions, his discontent pooled into anger at the lady he'd foolishly tried to help.

Elizabeth circled round to come back. She was surprised to see the major's chestnut standing riderless in the road. She quickly rode back to the fence she'd just vaulted. Sliding to the ground on the road side, she left the horse in the woods.

"Major Shelton, are you all right?" Elizabeth's voice trembled just a little at the thought of what might have happened to the gentleman.

The young boy, not more than twelve and dressed in an old grey shirt and dirty pants, stood at the end of the cart, pointing at the hay. " 'm's safe 'n' sound in there."

Dashing around the end of the collapsed conveyance, Elizabeth halted, then bit her lip to keep from laughing. The soldier sat in the middle of the cart, hatless. Straw was sticking in his hair, in his jacket, and even out of the tops of his boots. His green eyes held a sparkling glint as he eyed her.

Imogene came round the corner at a modest canter and pulled her horse to a halt. She slid down beside Elizabeth, releasing a tiny giggle when she asked, "Are you unharmed, Roderick?"

"Yes, no thanks to Miss Fields." The major stood up and brushed straw from his hair, giving it the tousled look of a small boy's.

Placing her gloved hands upon her hips, Elizabeth protested. "How can I be responsible for your landing in that cart, sir?"

"I was attempting to save you."

Elizabeth laughed as she turned and walked to the wall behind which her horse stood. "But, Major, I told you last night that I was capable of taking care of myself. You would be well advised to heed what I say."

Imogene saw her brother's eyes darken as he watched the lady scramble up the stone fencing and remount her horse. She didn't want him to be angry with Miss Fields, for she liked the lady excessively. In truth, she suspected he was more disconcerted at losing his seat than angry with Elizabeth. " 'Tis of no importance what caused the accident, Roderick, only that you have come through unharmed."

The sounds of the others approaching caused the major to bridle his temper and agree with his sister. "As you say, my dear."

Sir Gordon and Miss Bradford came round the corner, followed by the carriage. The company drew to a halt, and Miss Langley called, "Was anyone hurt?"

Roderick, assuming as dignified a stance as possible under the circumstance, assured her he was fine. Then he picked up his hat from the roadway, and helped his sister back on her horse. He overheard Sir Gordon's soft voice as the man moved near the carriage and spoke to Miss Langley. "Some are reckless to a fault. I would guess the sister to be much like the brother. Not a good trait for one who must manage an estate."

Fixing an icy stare on the baronet, Roderick realized that Miss Fields's warning about the gentleman was correct. But it would do Imogene's cause no good to create a scene here, for the heiress seemed to be encouraging the dandy, as she sat in the carriage chuckling. Perhaps he should have a private conversation with Sir Gordon.

Turning to mount Orion, he saw Miss Fields eye him with continued amusement. Why did the chit get under his skin so? She was nothing like the tractable, proper women he usually admired. But he could not deny that she was intriguing. Too often he felt torn between wanting to shake her or kiss her, and he had no business doing either one.

Wishing to be away from the lady's disturbing presence, Roderick suggested that he and Sir Gordon might go to the village to find help for the lad whose cart was disabled.

Despite the baronet's protest, Miss Langley agreed, saying she would make certain the young ladies made it safely back to the Hall for it looked like it was darkening to rain.

Waiting until Miss Powers had successfully turned the carriage round and Miss Fields had found an opening in the fence to return to the roadway, Roderick watched the party make their way back towards Langley. Then he turned his gaze to Sir Gordon as they started for the village. "Well, sir, I am glad we have this time alone, for I have been wishing a word with you in private."

The dandy's face flushed and his eyes grew round. "With me, Major, I cannot imagine what we could have to discuss."

With a predatory grin, Roderick spoke with a voice as cold as granite. "Don't you?" He was going to enjoy dressing down the fop for his ungentlemanly conduct. It would do much to relieve his frustration over his fascination with the blue-eyed vicar's daughter.

# Five

The varying members of the company assembled that evening in the Yellow Saloon after dinner, with the exception of Miss Hartman. Declaring her nerves to be quite shattered after her experience with Reynard, Prudence opted to have a quiet dinner in her room.

Sir Gordon stood behind his cousin, eyeing Esmé's invited guests closely. Major Shelton was in a lighter mood as he stood with a half-smile on his face, watching his sister and Miss Fields walk about the room arm in arm. His sister was in high spirits as well, giggling childishly at whatever inanities she and her companion were discussing.

The baronet ground his teeth, remembering the warning the soldier had given him during the ride to the village. The man dared to advise him to cease ridiculing the young ladies in Miss Langley's presence. He'd soothed the soldier's ire with all the right words, but the major had underestimated his man.

Once back in his room, with the bolstering encouragement of Ryland, Sir Gordon decided he could avoid Shelton's rancor by leaving Miss Shelton out of his verbal attacks when her brother was present. He could probably dismiss that quarter as a threat altogether. After all, she was a flighty little baggage, having no polish or style and little to recommend her to Esmé.

This evening his targets would be the quiet Miss Powers and the fashionable Miss Bradford. The London beauty had been making a cake of herself much of the day, flirting with Major Shelton, a fact which tweaked the baronet's ego. Tonight, however, her mother had her well in hand, seated at the pianoforte and looking for a selection to entertain the party.

Shifting his elegantly attired frame, Sir Gordon eyed the vicar with a wicked gleam in his eyes. The sanctimonious old goat had accidentally aided his cause by giving Mrs. Bradford a tongue-lashing before dinner about the wastefulness of Society and those who cavorted within its realm. The rotund matron and her daughter had been speechless for a short while and now appeared to be avoiding the vicar's company.

Mr. Tyler, having cornered Miss Powers, was boring the chit with some tale, for she sat glassy-eyed. She was mutely nodding in agreement and stroking the head of Esmé's annoying dog.

The baronet knew what tack he would take to undermine each of the ladies. He would emphasize Julia's lack of conversation, for the chit became quite the inept stutterer if brought to the fore of any discussion. The only thing he'd seen that might impress Esmé about the girl was that the cursed little mutt seemed to like her.

He moved his gaze to Miss Bradford. With her he could criticize her extravagant wardrobe and her coquettish manners, although, he admitted to himself, she looked very dashing in a peach-coloured silk gown with Van Dyking on the sleeves and skirt. He felt a certain disappointment that she'd paid scant attention to him, for here, at least, was a lady he would not be embarrassed to have on his arm in Town.

His plan set, Sir Gordon strolled to the mantel so that Esmé might observe his elegance in a powder blue evening coat. He pulled out his snuff box and deftly opened it with a single flick of his thumb, knowing that his cousin was watching with admiration. As he reached in for a pinch, he quietly said, "Do you not think Miss Powers a mute little creature? I always wonder if that is due to shyness or a lack of any innate intelligence on—"

His arm was suddenly jarred sending a shower of snuff down the front of his white waistcoat.

"Oh, sir, how clumsy of me," Elizabeth said without the least bit of contrition. She'd kept a close eye on the baronet all evening. It was evident that he was about to act on his plot when he moved in front of his cousin. She'd gently maneuvered Imogene close enough and had overheard his spiteful words. She could not resist the opportunity to foil his slanderous speech.

"Upon my soul! 'Twas very clumsy, indeed." Sir Gordon pulled a handkerchief from his pocket and managed to dust much of the brown substance from his clothing. Seeing the troublesome chit intended to remain at Esmé's side, he rudely turned and stalked to the opposite end of the room to bide his time.

Roderick chanced to hear the cutting comment about Miss Powers, and stifled a smile as he observed Miss Fields at work. Fearless at defending her friend, she would be interesting to watch as she matched wits with the fop. She might even keep him from having to thrash the cad for ignoring his warning.

Elizabeth exchanged a few polite common places with Miss Langley before Miss Bradford arrived and claimed the heiress's attention. She and Imogene resumed their stroll. "I understand you were at school in Bath before coming to Langley Hall," she said, keeping a watchful eye on the baronet.

Imogene made a moue of displeasure. "With Roderick away at the war, there has been no place else for me to go, for our uncle refuses any communication with us. I always assumed that my brother would inherit the title, but now that the viscount is to marry and likely to produce an heir, we are left to fend for ourselves. I think perhaps I should consider offering my services as a governess."

Elizabeth cast a glance at the girl's elfin face, gingery red hair, and simple white muslin gown. Miss Shelton didn't look old enough to be out of the schoolroom much less thinking of teaching small children. "I would say you are a bit young to find a post of that kind. Could you not go and be with your brother? I know many women accompany their husbands and brothers to the wars."

Imogene's green eyes, perhaps a shade darker than her brother's, widened at the suggestion. "I should adore going to Portugal, but Roderick would never approve. He says that following the drum is no life for a lady. Why, when he was engaged to that dreadful Miss Martin who jilted him, he refused to consider . . ."

"He refused to consider . . ." Elizabeth prompted.

The girl blushed, looking over at her brother. "I don't think I should be telling you this. Roderick says that I am such a prattle-box."

"Then we shall speak of something else, for I would not want to see your brother giving you black looks as he is wont to do with me."

Imogene cocked her head to look at Elizabeth. "I hope you will not jump to any wrong conclusions about him. He is the best of fellows, but I think he is worried about me, not to mention having his heart broken by his fiancée last year. I fear she wounded him severely, for he declares he shall never marry."

Elizabeth changed the subject, but her gaze was drawn to the handsome soldier across the room, again dressed in his regimental jacket. She felt a sudden urge to go and comfort him for the wrongs done him by the unknown lady. Why, if she had a handsome gentleman who loved

her she would— She pushed the thought from her mind.
She could never abandon Ruth and Sarah. There was no
point in thinking about being in love. She threw herself
into a conversation about Miss Langley's fashionable
gown and the latest styles, and tried to put the soldier
from her mind.

Across the room Sir Gordon watched for another opportunity to get close to Miss Langley. When Aegis
brought the tea tray, the baronet rushed to move a table
close to his cousin, then took a position at her elbow to
observe the layout of the group.

Esmé questioned the butler as to why he was late. The
old man replied that Cook was not feeling the thing, what
with the cake she'd baked falling and the maid letting
the beef get overdone. Urging him to go appease the
temperamental woman, the heiress declared she preferred to serve her guests herself. The butler's loud voice
echoed in the saloon, "As you wish, madam."

Fortunately, Miss Fields offered to help pass around the
teacups, so Sir Gordon slid into the vacant seat on the
opposite side of the tray as the young lady took the first
cup to Mrs. Bradford.

"What other exciting things do you have planned for
your guests, cousin?"

Esmé smiled across the silver teapot. "I believe Prudence is making preparations for a ball at the end of the
visit. We shall try to manage a picnic, weather permitting,
and a visit to Harrowgate. Other than that, I want the
young ladies to spend time with me, meet the tenants,
and get to know the people of the neighborhood."

The baronet swung his quizzing glass back and forth
on a long black ribbon while Esmé handed another cup
of tea to Miss Fields. As the young lady moved away, Sir
Gordon continued, "I suppose it is best to leave them to
their own devices, for one must become accustomed to
the quiet of the country. It would never do to leave your

fortune to a young lady who couldn't abide being away from Town."

"True," Esmé replied, pouring out another cup. "But then Julia and Imogene have not been in Society, so I do not need to fear such from them."

Sir Gordon looked up to see Miss Fields's eyes trained on him. Remembering the snuff, he hurriedly said, "Yes, Miss Powers or Miss Shelton would be aptly suited for country life."

Elizabeth took the cup, smiling as she turned. She had clearly made an impression on the baronet. But she didn't like the idea of his slandering any of the other guests for his own purposes. It rankled her sense of fair play. She determined she would stop him from defaming any of the ladies. Perhaps even send him on his way, but how?

Having served the ladies, she returned to receive another cup. Just as she reached Miss Langley she heard Sir Gordon snidely saying, "One can clearly see that Miss Bradford is quite the darling of Society. Quite the little coquette, though. One wonders if she could handle the rigors of managing tenants and—"

Elizabeth had heard enough. Taking the cup of tea Miss Langley gave her, she thrust it toward Sir Gordon. "Your tea, sir." The cup teetered precariously before toppling straight into the gentleman's lap.

With a yelp, Sir Gordon bolted from his seat, sending the cup flying. By some miracle Elizabeth managed to grab the delicate china before it landed on the carpet. She heard a stifled giggle from Imogene as the baronet danced around in a circle declaring his clothes to be ruined. Elizabeth apologized profusely. She'd only meant to splash the disagreeable fop, not drench him.

"Here, sir, let me help you." Elizabeth picked up a napkin from the tray and tried to dry some of the spilled tea from his fashionable evening apparel.

Angrily Sir Gordon held out a slender white hand to keep the young lady at bay. His elegant garments were soaked. Torn between strangling Miss Fields and absenting himself from the room, his vanity won out. He apologized to his cousin and said he would make his good night.

After the baronet left, the party returned to quiet, genial conversations. Pouring the young lady a cup, Esmé noted Miss Fields's guilty expression. "Don't give it a thought child. The tea is quite tepid tonight. I shall have Prudence speak to Cook about it in the morning."

Elizabeth smiled, thankful for the kind words. Needing some time to gather her wits, she took her cup and settled in a chair by the window.

Major Shelton strolled up beside her. "That was an ingenious maneuver, Miss Fields. Short of planting him a facer, I don't think I could have done as well to silence the cad myself."

Elizabeth frowned at the gentleman. Her conscience bothered her. "But he might be injured. Besides, he did not get his tea. Do you think I should take him a cup and apologize once more?"

A smile played about his well-shaped mouth. "Seeing you with another cup of tea might be more than the makebate could handle. Unless he takes a chill from the drenching, it is doubtful this mild brew caused any harm."

After the major bowed and went to his sister's side, Elizabeth tested the tea. They were right, it was only warm. Why, Sir Gordon was a sly fox. He had merely been acting to get sympathy from his cousin. She gritted her teeth.

Knowing there was little she could do about Mondell tonight, she shifted her attention to the major. He'd actually praised her skill at forestalling the baronet's spiteful tongue. Not what she would have expected from the man who'd snapped at her after his accident. The soldier was a puzzle, blowing hot and cold with her.

Perhaps a broken heart did account for his behavior. But then, it did not concern her, or so she kept trying to convince herself as she finished her cup of tea.

Julia, finally escaping from Mr. Tyler's boring recitation, approached Elizabeth. "Don't tease yourself so about the accident, my dear."

Her sweet friend was oblivious to the undercurrents in the drawing room and didn't realize Elizabeth had deliberately spilled the tea. It was not in Julia's nature to do mischief, therefore she did not see the trait in others. Perhaps a warning was in order.

"Come to my room, for there is only Mrs. Bradford in that wing with me." Elizabeth rose and glanced at the corpulent widow shoving another sweet between her lips. "I am sure she will not leave here until all the macaroons and cakes are done, so we might speak in private."

When they said their good nights, Elizabeth noted the twinkle in Major Shelton's green eyes. She felt a sudden thrill shoot through her at the thought that she had put it there. He bowed slightly, and she dismissed the sensation as a momentary aberration. Avoiding another look into those mesmerizing orbs, she led her friend up to her chamber.

"Damme, Ryland!" Sir Gordon shouted. "Have a care, for 'tis quite painful."

The valet made no comment, but continued to rub ointment on the discoloured spots on the baronet's thighs. The servant wasn't sure if they were tea stains or true burns.

"Upon my soul, the woman is a menace." The gentleman shifted on the bed so his man might apply the salve to the spots on his right side.

"What's your scheme now, sir? Or are you keepin' to your plan?" Ryland never took his eyes from the task at hand, but he wanted to guide his master in the direction he believed the wisest course to take. He'd never thought this plan of deriding the young ladies would work, for Miss Langley was a knowing one despite being a female.

"Keep to my plan! Have you taken leave of your senses, man? The chit nearly gelded me with that cup of scalding tea."

The valet, finished with the salve, took a piece of white cloth from the water where it had been soaked, and placed it over the affected region. "You must devise a new strategy, sir. Can't let these creatures take what's rightfully yours. You've earned it, what with your marked attentions to your cousin."

Sir Gordon laid his head back on the pillow, allowing the cool material to soothe the tingling. He'd never been able to tolerate even the slightest pain. Though truth be told, his pride suffered more than the superficial injury to his thighs. His handsome face puckered in anguish. "You are right, as always, Ryland. But I cannot think at present, I am in so much misery."

Ryland resisted a snort, for he noted the marks on his master were barely visible as he removed the damp cloth. "Well, sir, I still think the best way to go is to court the young ladies. Watch and see which is most in favor with Miss Langley and make that one the object of your gallantries."

The baronet's eyes narrowed, and his mouth became a petulant line. "I don't like that idea one bit. Dearest Lady Jane is the female I have pledged to adore. To align myself with a nobody would do nothing for my standing in Society. Besides, it would be just like Esmé to change her mind after I was leg-shackled to one of the chits. Furthermore, not one 'em has taken the least notice of me except for Miss Shelton." He stopped for a moment before sulkily adding, "And she seemed more interested in what kind of carriage I own and going for a drive in the vehicle than in me."

"That's because you haven't gone out of your way to be pleasin' to the young ladies. Praise is the key, sir. A lady can't resist bein' told she's the fairest chit in the room. Rig yourself out in one of your finest outfits, and I'm sure you can turn the lot of 'em up sweet in a day or so. Why, you're a regular nonpareil, no doubt about it." Ryland often resorted to blatant flattery to accomplish his purpose with his master.

Sir Gordon bit pensively on his lower lip, pondering his valet's advice. He might marry the chit Esmé chose if he got the old lady's approval. Then he could safely leave her here. None of the gentlemen in the *ton* danced attendance on their wives unless they were foolish and thought themselves in love. Why, his own attachment to Lady Jane was more for the Society in which she moved than any true affection.

"Upon my soul, Ryland. You are right. Did my trunks arrive from Town?"

"They did, sir."

"Then I shall wear my new lilac coat in the morn—" The baronet stopped abruptly. Raising himself on one elbow, he asked, "You don't think Miss Fields will have any objections to my courting that little mouse, Julia? I tell you, Ryland, the Fields woman is dangerous to be around."

The valet gently pushed his master back onto the bed. Unlike Sir Gordon, Ryland knew the major was the one who posed the greatest threat if Mondell continued to slander the ladies, but he didn't deem it wise to tell the dandy such, for the baronet wasn't the bravest of fellows. "I see no reason for her to object. A plain little thin' like Miss Powers could use someone whisperin' pretty words in her ear. Might actually pluck up her confidence."

"Yes, yes, I shall be helping the chit." Sir Gordon settled back on the bed, pleased with his plan. He would shower the ladies with compliments and attention. Why, he would even toady old Mrs. Bradford, but under no circumstances would he get within ten feet of that vixen, Miss Fields.

"If that is all, I shall bid you good night, sir." The valet interrupted the baronet's thoughts.

"Night, Ryland. I don't think I shall be able to sleep so much as a wink, but I must get an early start. Likely I shall look a fright in the morning."

"Never fear, sir. We'll turn you out your usual immaculate self." He quietly put away his master's things, thinking himself well pleased with getting Sir Gordon to take the more sensible tack. A smile tugged at his usually sour mouth when he heard the dandy snoring as he exited the room for the night.

"You deliberately spilled the tea?" Julia's grey eyes grew round at the revelation from her friend. She turned on the bed and watched Elizabeth pace on the Oriental rug. "I declare, Lizzie, I think you are reverting to your former ways."

"Former ways?" Elizabeth paused, to eye Julia.

"Of being a sad romp, just like before you settled down to care for your sisters and brothers."

"I did not spill the cup as a jest. How can you think such?" But Elizabeth knew she might have done such a childish thing five years ago when she rarely gave a thought to anything but having fun. "Was I such a complete madcap back then?"

Julia slid off the bed and went to her friend. "I thought you the most dashing young lady in the parish. I always wished I had just some trace of your courage and flair.

Even Mama used to say if I had even a small part of your spark for life I should not be ignored by everyone."

Elizabeth angrily drew her friend to her in a hug. She blamed Lady Powers for much of Julia's shyness, what with her constant criticizing of her daughter. "What a terrible thing to say. Why everyone in Aylsham likes you." Elizabeth refrained from telling her friend what the village thought about the baroness and her pushing ways.

Julia laughed as Elizabeth led her to the chairs beside the window. "Mama means well. You cannot deny that I could use a little of your easy manners in company."

Taking a seat, Elizabeth relaxed. "I am certain you will become more comfortable with these people as you get to know them better. After all we have only been acquainted with them for two days."

"Some I would prefer not to know any better." Julia pulled at the ribbons on her pink gown, twisting them in her fingers. "Tonight I was forced to listen to Mr. Tyler and how he is guiding the Widow Stanley now that she is without a husband. Somehow I found myself cornered in the drawing room, listening for quite thirty minutes about a lady I know nothing of. I strongly considered throwing *myself* into the moat until you doused Sir Gordon."

"Don't worry about the vicar; it is the baronet you must have a care with. He is determined to get Miss Langley's legacy, and he has been slandering the three of you at every opportunity."

"Are you certain? 'Tis hard to believe that someone with such a handsome countenance could be so treacherous."

"Julia, don't tell me you have developed a tendre for that man-milliner. Why, he made the most cutting remarks to your cousin about each of you! And he actually had the impertinence to disparage you in my presence this morning."

"A tendre?" Julia rose and went to stand by the darkened windows, her back to Elizabeth. "I would never give my heart to a gentleman whose goal in life is to be the best-dressed man in the *ton*. I could only esteem a gentleman who has a kind and caring heart. A well-read, well-mannered gentleman who uses his abilities to make a contribution to others."

Elizabeth watched her friend as the girl stared out into the night. "You sound as if you already know such a gentleman."

"I-I do."

A dawning realization struck Elizabeth. With a sinking feeling, she rose and went to Julia. "You have fallen in love with my father's curate?"

"Yes," was the whispered response.

Elizabeth ached for her friend. Jacob Ritter was just the sort of man who would be prefect for her friend, and just the sort who, if left to his own devices, would never defy Lady Powers's objections to the match. "Has Mr. Ritter declared himself?"

"I-I know he loves me, but Mama . . ." She broke off and took a deep breath, knowing there was no reason to be nervous around her friend. "Mama is always so daunting to him that he knows his suit will not be considered as long as he is a penniless curate." Julia stared sadly at Elizabeth as a single tear rolled down her cheek.

Taking her friend's hand, Elizabeth led her back to the chairs. "Don't worry about Mr. Ritter. Look on the bright side of your situation. If you become Miss Langley's heir, then money will not be a consideration for you and Jacob. If, however, she chooses one of the other ladies, I should think that even someone with Jacob's strict scruples will come to your defense and remove you from your mother's hectoring."

Julia brushed a tear from her cheek, a light of hope shining in her eyes. "I had not thought of that. Do you truly believe that Jacob might be brave enough to go against my mother's wishes?"

Knowing that if the young man were to witness even half of what Elizabeth had seen over the years, he would remove his beloved from Lady Powers's clutches, she replied, "I believe he will, especially with my encouragement. But let us not give up on your cousin just yet. She has shown no preference for anyone."

"True. I find that I like her very much. We had a nice conversation during our carriage ride this morning. She was vastly amused by your incident with the major."

"Hopefully, she did not blame you or Imogene for our contretemps with the hay cart. If she does not choose you to be the one to inherit, I should very much hope that her selection is the major's sister, for her circumstances are little better than your own." Elizabeth pulled on a small thread at the seam of her gown as if it were the most important thing for her to do at the moment.

Julia watched her friend's studied nonchalance as she spoke of Major Shelton. She had noted the way Elizabeth's eyes lit when they came to rest on the handsome gentleman. Julia knew her childhood companion would be adventuresome enough to make an excellent soldier's wife. Now if she would get past her notion that she must help her father raise his family . . . It was an argument they'd many times.

Knowing it would do no good to openly encourage Elizabeth to pursue the officer, Julia took a different approach. "Miss Bradford seems intrigued by Major Shelton. Perhaps if he had a wife like Myra, then he wouldn't have to worry about leaving Imogene alone when he returned to the Peninsula."

Elizabeth's eyes flashed fire. She very much disliked the way the London miss simpered and flirted with the major. "Myra Bradford would make a terrible wife for a soldier. She is just amusing herself with Major Shelton.

Can you see her aligning herself with a gentleman who has only his army pay? Why the gown she wore tonight would probably be half a year's funds for him."

Julia turned her head so that her friend could not see the amusement sparkling in her eyes. "But Cousin Esmé might choose her to be the Langley heiress, then she might follow her heart. Love often strikes the most mismatched persons. There is simply no accounting for what captivates two people when they meet."

Suddenly restless, Elizabeth rose and walked to the dressing table where her brushes lay. She picked up one and began to play with the curls about her face. Did the major prefer Miss Bradford's blond colouring to her own dark curls? Dark hair was rarely the fashion.

Or was he flattered by that lady's breathy compliments and fluttering eyes? Tossing the brush back onto the dressing table she pushed the thoughts from her mind. He was probably thinking more of his sister at a time like this than wishing to begin a romance.

"I don't know how we come to be talking about Major Shelton. 'Tis all moot anyway since Imogene says he intends never to marry. Our main worry should be Sir Gordon and what he is going to do next. You can be certain he has not abandoned his quest because I set him dancing like a caper-merchant."

Julia laughed. "Elizabeth, you cannot believe that Cousin Esmé is such a fool she does not see what he would be about in slandering each of us."

"I am certain she is no fool, Julia. In truth, I am coming to believe that she is merely amusing herself with the lot of us. She is looking for someone to bequeath her fortune to, but in the interim she is enjoying all the machinations swirling about under the surface."

"Machinations? That sounds so sinister." Julia shuddered as she watched her friend.

Elizabeth arched one delicate brow. "Nothing so dark,

I hope. Perhaps I should have said antics. Whatever the word, I believe your cousin is being highly entertained."

"She does seem to have a lively sense of humor." Julia yawned. "I fear I am quite fatigued. Unless you have something else you think I should know, I shall bid you good night."

Elizabeth said good night, promising to rise early. Later, as she lay in bed, she worried about Julia's thwarted desire of marriage. She hoped that she hadn't misled her friend about her chances for a future with Jacob. She would have to come up with some plan to encourage the shy cleric to pursue the lady he loved.

Thoughts of marriage caused the face of the major to flash into her mind. She was flooded with the memory of the twinkle in the major's green eyes as they left the drawing room. The man was simply too engaging by far to dismiss as a threat to her heart. She simply must do better at removing thoughts of him from her mind, she thought, turning onto her side.

"Remember, Papa needs me. Remember, Sarah and Ruth are motherless. Remember, you have a duty." She kept repeating those phrases as she drifted into sleep.

# Six

Never his best before noon, Sir Gordon was in a surly mood as he drank the coffee his valet brought long before the sun's rays began to warm the fields in the West Riding of Yorkshire. Silence reigned in his bedchamber when the baronet rose and began his toilette, for Ryland knew his master preferred no idle chatter in the mornings. Aware that Sir Gordon was not looking forward to his mission, the servant wisely determined to make the gentleman look his best.

With a sigh, the baronet donned his lilac morning coat over the matching white waistcoat emblazoned with tiny lilac flowers with yellow centers. Palest marigold pantaloons already encased his well-shaped legs. Finally he tugged on champagne-polished Hessians, just recently delivered from Hoby, with two small gold tassels on each boot.

"If I am not bein' too bold, sir, you shall have all the ladies taking a fancy to you if you but put yourself to the task."

"All? I hope not. Just the one to whom Esmé intends to leave her fortune." Sir Gordon shot Ryland a sour look.

The baronet sauntered across the room with an air of indifference to observe himself in the cheval mirror in the corner. His mood brightened considerably at the splendid sight. As he tweaked a blond curl into place, his confidence soared. What female could resist him at his fashionable best?

A jaunty kick to his step, he bid his valet to stay alert to any opportunity to advance his cause and exited the chamber. He made his way to the Great Hall, where he intended to lay in wait for the first young lady to venture down. She would fall victim to his considerable charm.

The hall was empty except for the footman on duty who eyed the baronet suspiciously. Some of the maids might be all aflutter over the handsome young man and his smarmy valet, but James thought it best to keep a careful eye on the cove. He knew a muckworm when he saw one and was only surprised that valuable articles hadn't turned up missing after each of the man's visits.

Sir Gordon circled the large entry as if he were inspecting the pieces of art and statuary which decorated the antechamber. In truth he kept a close watch on the stairs, hoping to waylay one of the ladies on her way to breakfast.

Unfortunately in his eagerness to begin, he'd risen long before those of the house party. The time lengthened into thirty minutes without a glimpse of his prey. He grew tired of walking and found a place that gave the best vantage point of the stairs. The spot was opposite an oversized mirror, in which he might best admire his person to relieve his boredom.

James resisted a snort as he watched the fop pose and posture in front of the looking glass. What was the lounger up to, and did it mean something bad for his mistress? The footman had no idea, but he vowed to keep his peepers on the fellow.

A movement in the hallway caught James's eye and he spied Miss Hartman, busy as always with her morning duties. He stood a little straighter not wishing to get a scold from the old tartar.

"Sir Gordon, is there something you wish?"

The baronet jumped at the peevish voice of his cousin's drab companion. He'd been so engrossed in admiring his new rig that he'd not seen the old harpy enter from the rear hall. Regaining his composure, he gave her his most winning smile. "Good morning, Miss Hartman. We missed your charming company last evening. I hope you have recovered your good health."

"I am well enough." The lady, immune to sweet words spoken by handsome gentlemen, watched Sir Gordon, convinced he was contemplating the possibility of seduction of one of the young ladies. Was that not what all young men thought about? She felt it her duty to protect the innocents while they were at Langley since Esmé was so naive. "Why do you stand here in the hall, sir?"

Sir Gordon gave the spinster another practiced smile. "I am waiting for Ryland to bring my gloves. I thought I might go for a stroll along the river's edge this fine morning."

Prudence's eyes narrowed. This young man was no more fond of nature than the Prince Regent was reputed to be fond of his wife, Princess Caroline. Turning to straighten a milky green jade dragon from the Tang period which looked poised to fly at Sir Gordon, she nonchalantly asked, "Do you go alone?"

"I fear I must, for there are no others about this fine morning."

Remembering her duties awaited and that Reynard might escape the footman again, she looked back at the young dandy. "Then I hope you enjoy your walk, sir. Pray excuse me, for I have much to do."

Sir Gordon watched the woman go up the stairs and disappear from sight. How Esmé put up with the creature was beyond him. Dismissing her from his thoughts, he strolled to the opposite side of the hall to admire a large silver urn with chinoiserie decoration, wondering what it was worth. The rapid click of heels on marble alerted him that someone approached.

Miss Imogene Shelton came down the long stairway at a brisk gait, as if she were skipping down some country lane. Sir Gordon resisted the urge to reprimand her. Instead, he stepped forward to greet the child, for that was how she appeared in her simple white morning gown.

"Good morning, Miss Shelton. You seem in excellent spirits."

Imogene came to a sudden halt, a blush warming her cheeks. Here was a handsome gentleman wishing to speak with her, and she'd been dashing about like a hoyden. She knew she should be flattered by this good fortune, but she only felt the foolish tendency to giggle. "Good morning, Sir Gordon. Are you recovered from your accident of last evening?"

"Completely. I must say that you are looking especially lovely this morning. I always say that white becomes a young lady better than any other colour."

Having always longed for dresses in deep reds and greens, Imogene merely smiled. "I shall defer to your superior knowledge, sir."

"I hoped to entice you into taking a ride in my curricle this afternoon, if you should like?"

Imogene's green eyes sparkled at the thought. "I should love to . . ." Suddenly remembering Roderick's anger over her last outing with a gentleman in a carriage, she bit at her lip, a frown marring her pretty features. ". . . But I don't think my brother would permit me to join you."

The baronet was not to be so easily defeated. "Might I recommend that you apply to our cousin for permission, for will she not be your guardian after your brother leaves for Portugal? Then should Major Shelton prove disagreeable, you might say you had Cousin Esmé's approval."

"No, Sir Gordon, I shall not try and force my brother

to agree to an outing of which he does not approve. I shall only accompany you if Roderick gives his permission." Imogene frowned at the baronet. She well knew her brother could not be manipulated, not that she hadn't tried.

"Then it will be as your brother decides, Miss Shelton." Surprised at the chit's resolve to obey the major, Sir Gordon knew better than to make an issue of the matter. "Perhaps you would enjoy a walk in one of our cousin's many fine gardens, should your brother refuse his consent to the outing?"

"I don't think I need ask my brother's permission for a stroll in the gardens, but if the weather holds fine, I would prefer to ride about the countryside, sir."

"Then I shall anxiously await knowing if you will allow me to tool you about or merely accompany you on a walk."

Sir Gordon offered the young lady his arm to escort her to the breakfast parlour. He thought he'd made a good beginning with the girl beside him. He didn't want to be too attentive so soon, for it was anyone's guess which of the young ladies Cousin Esmé might choose. It would never do to put all his efforts into the wrong chit.

Leading Miss Shelton down the hall, he inquired of her taste in reading. Giggling, she quickly professed a fondness for Minerva Press novels. Sir Gordon felt excessively pleased with himself, for that was just what he'd expected from a schoolroom miss.


The typically changeable English weather failed to oblige Sir Gordon with his plans to awe Miss Shelton with his handling of the ribbons. By nine o'clock the skies had gone grey, and within the hour rain had begun to fall as it can only in a summer storm. Imogene, her nerve failing

her, never got around to asking her brother's permission
before the deluge.

After the morning meal the members of the house
party had scattered throughout the house, amusing themselves on their own. Miss Langley informed them that she
intended to return to her rooms for the day, the rain
always making her arthritis worse. She had invited Miss
Bradford up to read to her.

Imogene trailed after her brother to the library where
she sat on a window seat peering out at the downpour.
Every so often a bored little sigh escaped her, as she remembered where she might have been.

Roderick looked up from the copy of Denon's transla-
tion of *Travels in Upper and Lower Egypt* he'd found earlier.
He knew his sister was restless, but made no comment.
He'd suggested several books to her, but she'd declared
them not to her taste and had settled by a tall window
with diamond-cut quarries. He was certain she would
soon tire of staring out at the storm and find something
to amuse herself.

Imogene sighed. "Rain, rain, rain. I do so dislike the
rain, for one is required to remain indoors."

"You sound as if you had had plans for an outing."
Roderick eyed her curiously.

"N-No, but if someone were to ask me to go driving,
would you object?" Imogene looked shyly at him.

Remembering the envious glances Imogene had cast at
Miss Powers as she'd tooled Miss Langley's carriage,
Roderick mistook his sister's question. He'd recognized
a superior driver in the lady and knew he had nothing
to fear. "If you take a groom along, I would have no
objections"

"Thank you, Roderick. You are the best of brothers."
Imogene sat back, pleased she'd gotten her wish. But
looking out at the weather, she knew it wasn't likely she
would go today. With a sigh, she slumped back against

the wall and began to idly tap at the lead strips between the quarries, causing the droplets to run together and roll faster down the glass.

The tapping soon annoyed Roderick despite his considerable patience. "Surely you did not sit by the window at Mrs. Johnson's and waste the whole day. Why not play a game of some kind?"

"By myself?"

"You used to play jackstraws for hours on end by yourself, as I remember."

"Jackstraws! I am not a child anymore to be so easily amused by mindlessly picking up straws." Imogene raised her chin indignantly at her brother's suggestion. Then she turned back to the window to stare out. "Besides, Cousin Esmé is not likely to have such a game here, since she had no children."

"Perchance one of the other young ladies might play something with you. They are most likely as restless as you." Roderick glanced down at the illustration by Denon of a Sphinx being measured, sure his sister would prefer the livelier company of Miss Fields—or one of the others. He could not envision that young lady sitting quietly bored during a summer storm.

Thoughts of the beautiful lady caused his mind to stray from the Frenchman's tales of his travels, and he found himself staring at the bright candles lit to relieve the gloom of the day. She'd been rather quiet at breakfast and had almost appeared to avoid looking at him. Had he said or done something to offend her last evening? he wondered.

A smile touched his lips. More likely she was planning something to bring attention to the shy Miss Powers. He was glad that Imogene did not suffer from such timorous behavior in company.

His sister interrupted his thoughts. "Roderick, do you

think that Cousin Esmé has shown a preference for Miss
Bradford by inviting *her* up to read?"

"I think your cousin is trying to get to know you each
better, and one does that best in privacy."

"Do you think Miss Bradford pretty?"

With a sigh, Roderick realized he would get little
chance to read with his garrulous sister present. "She has
a pleasing countenance. I would say that on the whole
Miss Langley has an exceptionally handsome family." But
his own thoughts were of Miss Fields's beauty.

"Myra is quite the flirt. I wonder if she is like that with
most men, or only handsome ones in uniform." Imogene
watched the expression on her brother's face as she mentioned the lady's preference for him. Roderick's indifference to Miss Bradford had caused Imogene to worry for
him. She could not bear the thought that his dreadful
experience with the feckless Miss Martin had turned his
thoughts from marriage so completely.

"The lady's conduct is not of the least import to us,
my dear. We shall likely never see any of these people
again, should you not receive Miss Langley's inheritance."
Roderick felt a sudden twist in his heart at the thought
of not seeing one of the ladies again.

"What if you have stolen Miss Bradford's heart? Could
you not consider her as a wife? I am certain she has a
very good chance of winning Cousin Esmé's approval with
her air of sophistication and her beauty." The elfin-faced
girl looked hopefully at her brother.

"I have not the least interest in Miss Bradford or marriage to any other woman, Imogene." Roderick's biting
tone clearly showed he wished the subject closed.

Imogene sighed, then turned back to the rain-streaked
window. " 'Tis probably for the best since I don't think
her mother approves of you. Maybe because of the dangers inherent in your being a soldier?"

Looking over at his sister, Roderick regretted his sharp

reply. He noted how pretty she appeared in her white muslin gown with ruffles at the sleeves and collar. She looked as innocent as she sounded. "More likely she does not wish her daughter to marry a man with only his military pay, child. No parent or guardian would encourage such a match. I think Mrs. Bradford will accept no less than a title for her daughter."

"But if Myra were to get Cousin Esmé's legacy, then you might marry her and not have to worry about—"

"Genie." Roderick snapped the book shut, putting the volume aside. He rose and went to his sister, "You are not still trying to play matchmaker for me, are you?"

"I would never encourage you to marry only for money, but if you were to develop a tendre for such a lady, there would be nothing wrong with marrying for love. You are the heir to a viscount, which might count for something with her mama." Imogene took her brother's hand as he stood before her. She did not particularly like Myra, but if Roderick did, she might come to care for the lady.

Squeezing his sister's hand, he smiled. "Don't get your hopes up that there will ever be a match between myself and Miss Bradford. In truth, I find her more an annoyance than an attraction. Besides, with the Langley fortune, she could look in the highest reaches of the peerage for a husband, and I am certain her mother will see that she does."

Imogene sighed. "I suppose you are right. She is not the lady *I* would have chosen for you, but she is forever hanging on your arm and I thought . . . Well never mind."

At that moment the door opened and Elizabeth entered the room to see Major Shelton and his sister in deep conversation. Dismayed at seeing the man who was so disturbing her thoughts, she meant to leave. "Pray forgive me. I did not know that anyone was here. I shall return later, for it is not a pressing matter. I merely wished to exchange a book."

Roderick put up a staying hand. "Don't leave, Miss Fields. My sister and I were just having a typical brother and sister disagreement about nothing important. I am sure you are quite familiar with such discussions."

Closing the door, Elizabeth smiled, fondly remembering her disputes with her own brothers. "That I am, Major. But it cannot have been much of a disagreement, for there are no books lying about that you two hurled at each other."

Imogene giggled. "Have you actually thrown a book at your brothers?"

"To be sure, in my untamed youth. I highly recommend *The Rise and Fall of the Roman Empire*. It is just light enough to easily toss, but heavy enough to bring an annoying twelve-year-old to his knees."

As they all laughed, Roderick said, "I think I begin to pity you poor brothers, Miss Fields."

"You needn't, sir, for I assure you they gave as good as they got."

At that moment the door opened and Miss Hartman entered the library, looking sourly at the trio. "Miss Shelton, your cousin desires that you join her in her apartments."

Imogene started to her feet, giving her brother a triumphant glance. In a whispered undertone, she said, "I shall remember my manners and my tongue."

Roderick watched his sister dash from the room as if she'd received an invitation to a ball. He was glad she would have something to occupy her on such a gloomy day, and he was certain that Miss Langley could not resist his endearing sister.

Miss Hartman stood in the doorway a few moments longer. "Miss Fields, would you care to join me in the Yellow Saloon?"

"Thank you, no. I merely came to exchange my book and then I shall join Julia in the Orangery." Elizabeth avoided looking at the major, fearing she would laugh at Miss Hartman's obvious ploy to remove her from his presence.

Prudence Hartman's eyes narrowed as she shot the soldier a warning glare to be on his best behavior. "There is a footman on duty should you need anything, my dear."

So saying, the lady exited the room, leaving the library door wide open.

Elizabeth, not wishing to burst into a peal of laughter which the companion might hear, walked to the shelves and returned the book she'd selected the day before. Behind her, she heard the major's soft chuckle which sent a shiver of pleasure through her.

Roderick leaned against the window frame, admiring the white arch of the lady's slender neck as she gazed up looking for a book. "Miss Hartman is greatly deluding herself that you are the one in danger from me."

Elizabeth pulled a volume from the shelf, with little thought to what she'd selected as her heart hammered at the major's teasing tone. "Is she?"

"If I were so imprudent as to cross the line with a lady like yourself, I have no doubt that my sister would return to find me buried beneath a pile of books, the finest literature. They, of course, being the very best to use as tools of defense for their size and ability at sailage."

Elizabeth, blue eyes twinkling, turned back to the gentleman. "I don't think you have anything to worry about from me or Miss Langley's books. You might rest easy on that thought. I have long since learned to control my more volatile emotions. If you will excuse me, Julia awaits my return."

Elizabeth exited the library, wondering if she truly had learned to control her emotions. If so, why did the major always leave her trembling with breathless excitement?

Pushing the disturbing thoughts from her mind, she hurried down the hallway to the Orangery which was situated on the west side of the house to get the best vantage of the afternoon sun on a winter day. During the summer the citrus-filled room got little use except for such rainy days.

Opening the door, she checked at the sight which greeted her. There, sitting on a marble bench amid the potted flowers and orange trees, were Julia and Sir Gordon. The gentleman was leaning close to her friend in the most intimate way.

Julia started up, relief showing in her eyes. "Elizabeth, I thought you would never return."

Sir Gordon rose and took a step away from the lady when he saw Miss Fields. He'd managed to avoid being around the woman most of the morning, and he knew he could no longer sit making eyes at Miss Powers with her friend glaring at him. "I have just remembered I must go speak with my cousin. Pray excuse me, ladies."

Elizabeth watched him nervously edge past her and enter the house. Going to her friend, she could see that Julia was very discomposed. "What has he been about now?"

"Sir Gordon just spent the last quarter of an hour trying to convince me that I am the most enchanting female of his acquaintance. It was most disconcerting, and I cannot say that I like being the object of his gallantries." Julia clutched the book she'd been reading to her.

Elizabeth stared thoughtfully at the half-grown green oranges on the tree. What new tack was this to be making up to her friend? Looking back at Julia, she offered a possible explanation. "Perhaps he was merely trying to make amends for the dreadful things he has been saying about you and the others."

Julia shook her head. "You know, Lizzie, that was my first thought, but as he continued to utter the most patently false compliments about me, I suddenly felt I was being courted."

"Courted? You think Sir Gordon has developed a tendre for you?" Elizabeth's voice was full of doubt for she was suspicious that a London swell like the baronet would be making up to an unfashionable country-bred miss like Julia, despite all her friend's many fine qualities.

"Not in the least, for I am not that easily taken in by pretty words and a handsome face. Besides, I haven't forgotten what you told me about the gentleman the other night. I remembered that his sole reason for being here was my cousin's fortune. 'Tis my belief that you convinced him to cease his slandering with that spilled cup of tea, for one can see that his attire takes up a great deal of his thought. But if he still wants to be Cousin Esmé's heir, and I believe he does, then it occurred to me that perhaps the gentleman intends to marry the next Langley heiress, whichever lady that may be."

Elizabeth looked at Julia with dawning realization. "Why, that would explain his change in demeanor at breakfast. He positively dangled after Imogene at the table, but I put it down to his fear that the major might plant him a facer if he continued to defame Miss Shelton."

"Only think, Lizzie, since he does not know which of us is to inherit, he will have to make up to three ladies at the same time." Julia's grey eyes grew round at the prospect. "That should prove wearing even for the dashing Sir Gordon."

Nodding her head, Elizabeth took a seat on the bench and Julia joined her, both silent with their own thoughts at the new turn of events. The very absurdity of such a plan made Elizabeth want to laugh until she gave the matter more reflection. Miss Langley was clearly determined to bequeath her fortune to a female. Therefore, marriage *was* the only way the baronet could get his hands on the legacy.

Elizabeth had no fear that her friend might fall victim to the fop's flattery, but what about an innocent like Imogene? Perhaps she should warn the major, for she would not wish to see his sister taken only for the Langley fortune.

The door opened, interrupting her thoughts A footman had arrived with mail for the young ladies. Elizabeth received short notes from her sisters, full of praises for Miss Wade, enclosed in a longer missive from her father, assuring her all was well in her absence.

Julia's letter was from her mother. The missive was filled with admonishments not to disappoint, leaving the young lady in a dark and somber mood.

Elizabeth spent much of the afternoon restoring her friend's good humor. Later, in her room to change for dinner, she pulled out her own letter, rereading the messages from her sisters. Their enthusiasm at having Miss Wade at the vicarage made Elizabeth question her own role in the household. Then she assured herself her sisters were but trying to ease her worries about them while she was away. With her anxiety about her family and Julia, Elizabeth completely forgot her wish to warn the major of what appeared to be Sir Gordon's latest scheme.

Major Shelton stepped out onto the rain-washed flagstone of the terrace outside the Egyptian Drawing Room, breathing deeply of the cool damp air. The only sounds in the darkness were the slow dripping of water from the nearby trees onto the stone walkway and the noises made by the small night creatures who welcomed a respite from the deluge.

Although it was scarcely after half-past ten, some members of the party had already retired for the evening. Only

Miss Langley, Sir Gordon, Mrs. Bradford, and her daughter were still engaged in playing whist in the Yellow Saloon. Roderick had made a quiet escape to come out and exercise his healing leg which had grown cramped from the long day of inactivity.

Turning, he limped toward the front of the Hall. He halted abruptly when he spied someone seated on a stone bench in the darkness. In the silvery moonlight he could clearly make out the lovely face that seemed too often to haunt him.

"Good evening, Miss Fields. I thought you had retired for the night."

"I meant to, but the moonlight beckoned me. Have you ever noticed how clearly one can think in the darkness?" Elizabeth looked up at the major, admiring the line of his jaw illuminated by the dim light spilling from the windows of the drawing room.

"Plotting a new campaign for Miss Powers to use to win the legacy?" Roderick smiled.

"Perhaps," Elizabeth bantered. "But as you so aptly reminded me, it would never do to reveal my plans."

"True, for the key to a good strategy is always surprise."

"I shall take your word for that, sir." The only surprise in Elizabeth's life was the way she felt when the major was near. As if all her nerves were tingling, she thought. She ought to retire, despite her desire to stay and talk with the gentleman. "The cool air has been most enjoyable, but I am beginning to feel tired, so I shall bid you good night."

"Miss Fields, I should thank you for your assistance in putting a stop to Sir Gordon's slander of Imogene and the others." Roderick had noted the baronet was on his best behavior this evening, being agreeable to everyone.

Elizabeth was suddenly reminded that she wished to speak to the major about his sister. "Sir, don't thank me prematurely. I think the gentleman has come up with a new ploy. I believe he intends to marry the lady who is designated the future heiress."

Roderick frowned. "Are you certain?"

"Not absolutely, but I suspect that is his plan. Julia said he spent his time with her this morning casting out lures in the most outrageous manner. Why, before you came to the breakfast parlour, he was openly flirting with Imogene. It is all quite subtle, but why else would he suddenly make himself agreeable to the ladies?"

"Why else, indeed?" Roderick replied thoughtfully, aware of the alluringly intoxicating scent that wafted from the lady.

Elizabeth stepped closer, laying a hand upon the gentleman's arm. "I don't fear that Julia might be taken in, but do you think your sister . . . ?" Her voice trailed off as she looked breathlessly up into his handsome face. Despite the dimness of the moonlight, she could see his features in the glow of light from the windows. The feel of his muscular arm through the cloth set her heart racing.

Roderick sensed the warmth of her hand and stared down at her beautiful upturned face. A sudden wish to take her in his arms overwhelmed him. Hoarsely, he said, "I shall take care . . . to speak with her about the matter."

Elizabeth dropped her hand and took a step back. How had she come to lose so much control over her emotions? She would go see Julia. Perhaps her friend could convince her that she was merely bewitched by a red uniform. "Good night, Major."

"Good night, Miss Field." The major turned and walked to the edge of the terrace, struggling to get his own emotions under control.

He heard the door close behind him. What madness possessed him when he was around Elizabeth Fields? He couldn't put a name to it, he only knew that he wanted

her in a way that he'd never known before. This wouldn't
do. He already had to worry about leaving his sister behind. He wouldn't add a wife to his list of concerns.

Thoughts of Imogene suddenly made him realize that
she was in a greater danger from Sir Gordon than before.
He wouldn't allow that gentleman to marry his sister just
to get ahold of the Langley fortune. The fop would make
her life a misery.

The sound of the door again opening behind him
caused his heart to race. Was Elizabeth back? Roderick
turned, hoping that she'd returned and dreading that
he'd lose all rational thought in her presence.

But it was not the enchanting Elizabeth. He was startled
to see Mr. Tyler coming to join him, the long white runners of his clerical collar glowing luminously in the moonlight.

"There you are, Major. I was certain a soldier would
not be for his bed so early."

"I merely wanted a little fresh air before I retired, sir.
I am not used to being idle during the day." Roderick
turned to stare out in the darkness as the vicar came and
stood beside him.

"There is nothing like the freshness of the countryside
after a good rain. A renewal of the land and a helping
of things to grow. Farming is perhaps the noblest thing
one can do to help mankind. God lends a helping hand
with rain." The older man seemed surprisingly subdued
this evening.

"Nature washing away the transgressions we commit
against the land?" Roderick was full of his own disturbed
thoughts, but he sensed the cleric wanted to converse
and was surprised he'd chosen him.

Mr. Tyler chuckled. "Very likely." The gentleman fell
silent for a few moments, then cleared his throat. "Have
you ever had cause to regret choosing the army as your
career, sir?"

Roderick turned to look at him, but with their backs turned to the drawing room, shadows covered the vicar's face, keeping his expression hidden. Did he have any regrets? Yes, he did. One immense regret. He knew that despite the death and destruction at Badajoz and even in earlier encounters with the French, that was not what caused his regret, for he was fighting for his country. "I have, sir. Every time I must sail away and leave my sister in the care of strangers. But I know that I had not the temperament for the church or the law."

"So, you think one must satisfy one's own wishes in regard to profession." The vicar reached out and plucked a dead leaf from the stone balustrade where they stood, twirling it idly between his fingers.

"I do, for how can you successfully execute your duties, if you don't choose something which gives you satisfaction, sir? If one is unhappy with one's profession, then I would think one would not be very good at the position."

Mr. Tyler nodded his head. "I would say you are correct, sir." The vicar suddenly tossed the leaf over the stone rail into the shrubbery. "I must be going for it is quite late, Major."

Roderick bid the gentleman good night, wondering what troubled the fellow. Knowing that he had difficulties of his own, he pushed thoughts of the clergyman from his mind. He felt a pressing need to speak with Imogene tonight. She was too vulnerable to the practiced advances of a dandy like Sir Gordon, and clearly the man had already begun his maneuver.

Entering the house, he made his way towards his sister's room. He passed the Yellow Saloon. Hearing Sir Gordon's low voice and then laughter from the ladies, he suppressed an urge to enter the room and take the baronet by his stiff collar to boot him out of the Hall completely. The man, after all, was Esmé's cousin as well, and she would not take kindly to Roderick's interfering with her guest.

He went straight to his sister's room instead. At least he had some measure of control over her. About to knock on the door, he was startled by hearing Imogene's muffled scream.

# Seven

Roderick threw open the door. "Genie, what's wrong?"

The chamber lay in near darkness except for a single candle burning beside the bed. The covers Imogene clutched to her mouth muffled her screams which had ceased upon his entrance.

Seeing her brother, she raised a trembling hand to point at a darkened corner of her large room.

Even as he'd spoken, a movement caught Roderick's eye. A thin white shape with arms swaying gracefully up and down suddenly froze. Then the apparition twirled around and disappeared into the darkness created by an oversized wardrobe.

"Oooooh, Roderick, thank heavens you have come." Imogene's voice quavered as she extended a hand to him.

The major quickly crossed the room to reassure himself that his sister was unharmed by the nocturnal visitor. "Who was that?"

"Who? Why, it was a-a ghost of some dead relative of Cousin Esmé's come back to haunt the place. Maybe one who expired in this very room." Imogene searched the room with a wide-eyed gaze as if she expected to see a body.

"Ghost?" Even though he'd seen the thing, Roderick did not believe it to be any ancestral specter. "Balderdash!

Have any of the servants mentioned the Hall being haunted?"

"N-No doubt my cousin warned them not to speak of such things. She would not wish to frighten us all away." Imogene felt safe now that her brother was with her, but she could see the doubt in his face. "I tell you it was a ghost. It made the most dreadful moaning noise when it first appeared."

"Appeared! More likely your invader walked into the room," Roderick scoffed. He then picked up the single candle from the bedside table to examine the place where the "spirit" had been. Illuminating the dark corner, he asked, "So you think you were visited by a ghost? A very dense fellow that has to use a door?" He gestured at the entry which had been invisible in the darkness.

The major opened the portal to reveal an empty dressing room. Holding the candle high, he could see a door at the opposite end which connected with an adjoining chamber. He strode to the second door and was about to open it when he heard his frightened sister wail.

"Please don't leave me in the dark," she begged.

He wanted to pursue the intruder, but concern for Imogene stayed him. Returning to her chamber, Roderick was struck by how young and vulnerable she looked sitting in the large fourposter. Her gingery red hair streamed out from under a plain white bed cap, and her green eyes were wide with terror. Sitting with her covers clutched in a death grip, no doubt one "Boo" would send her scurrying beneath the bed.

He realized in such a frightened state Imogene wouldn't listen to reason. Going to her, he picked up the wrapper which lay at the end of the bed. "Come, we shall trade rooms for tonight. Shall I ring for a maid to stay with you?"

Imogene scooted from the bed, slipping into the proffered garment. "I-I think I shall be fine in your room if I might keep a candle burning during the night."

Roderick kissed his sister on top of her head. "You might have an entire branch of candles if that is what you wish, my dear."

Some fifteen minutes later, after settling Imogene comfortably in his room, he returned to his sister's chamber. Standing in the center of the room, the single candle lighting the door through which he was certain the pretend spirit had escaped, he pondered who would wish to frighten his sister.

Could Sir Gordon be behind the ghostly visit? While he knew the baronet himself still played cards, Roderick realized that the man's valet might be capable of such a trick. But something about the supposed specter nagged at Roderick's thoughts.

The "ghost" had appeared very willowy in shape and graceful in movement, not characteristics he would attribute to Sir Gordon's valet or to any other male. Suddenly it came to him. Why, the masquerading spirit had to have been a woman!

The thought sent him reeling. A gently bred female sneaking about the halls at night and slipping into people's bedchambers. No lady would do something so unconventional, so lacking in . . . But even as his mind rejected the possibility, he knew just such a lady. Had he not seen her sitting with her bare feet in the moat? Had she not boldly dumped a cup of tea onto Sir Gordon when the man threatened her friend's chance at the inheritance? Had her own friend not told him the lady was renowned for outrageous antics in her past?

It must have been Miss Fields. The only other possibilities were Miss Powers and Miss Hartman, for they, too, had retired early. Neither lady seemed to have the fortitude or the sheer effrontery to engage in such a prank.

No, only the audacious, unconventional Miss Elizabeth Fields would dare such a scandalous stunt.

As the major walked to the dressing-room door, his mind was in turmoil. He couldn't believe the lady would go to such extremes to frighten his sister away. But his powers of reason told him it was so. He passed through the small dressing chamber and entered the bedroom on the opposite side, his anger building by the minute. The room was similar to the one where his sister had slept, only it was clearly unoccupied.

In truth, Roderick knew that he might have been amused by the lady's scheme if she hadn't made Imogene the object of her prank. A vision of Elizabeth's luminous blue eyes came to his mind, but he pushed the enticing picture away. There would be no more of such thoughts. She had declared war on him and his sister, and in the morning she would find that he was an able opponent.

He walked to the door to look into the hallway to see if anyone was about. Turning the handle, he was surprised to discover the door locked. How had she managed to do that, he wondered. He thoughtfully fingered the key which protruded from the lock before turning it to open the door.

The hallway was empty, but that didn't surprise him. Miss Fields was no fool. Not only was she beautiful, she was quite adept and clever as well. Not many women he knew possessed such traits. Again entering the room, he closed and then locked the portal.

Roderick puzzled over the locked door as he made his way back to his sister's chamber. An answer escaped him, but despite the question of how she'd managed to lock it after she'd left, he was no less convinced that Miss Fields was the ghost who'd visited his sister.

Certain that the lady wouldn't return, the major took no chances. He settled himself into a gold silk wingback chair, which he turned to face the dressing-room door.

Primed for a confrontation if she did reappear, he pre-pared for the long night ahead. Regardless, he would seek her out on the morrow and give her fair warning that he was not a man to be crossed.

The following morning dawned sunny and dry. Eliza-beth and Julia arrived for breakfast to discover much of the house party down before them. Only Miss Hartman, who never came to breakfast, and Miss Shelton appeared absent from the table.

After the young ladies exchanged greetings with the assembled company and were seated, Sir Gordon and Miss Bradford resumed their conversation with talk of events in London. Elizabeth paid scant attention, for she was very aware that the major had not taken his eyes from her since she'd remarked on his sister's absence.

Suddenly breaking into Miss Bradford's tale of meeting Prinny's brother, the Duke of York, on Bond Street, the major asked, "Miss Field, would you accompany me for a walk after breakfast? There is a matter I should like to discuss."

Elizabeth's heart raced as she looked up from her plate to see his compelling green eyes staring at her with an unfathomable look. At first all kinds of wildly romantic thoughts flooded her mind; then her calmer self took over. In their last encounter they had discussed Imogene. Surely he wanted some advice about how to handle Sir Gordon and his sister. "I should enjoy an outing, sir."

Despite spending nearly an hour with Julia last evening, trying to convince herself that the major was of no im-portance to her, Elizabeth couldn't help feeling flattered by his invitation. To have such a gentleman openly solicit her advice was very gratifying.

"Take her to the Enclosed Garden at the end of the Statue Walk," Esmé recommended.

Looking at the other members of the house party, Elizabeth greeted the curious glances of Sir Gordon, Mrs. Bradford, and Julia. Amusement was evident on Miss Langley's smiling face, but Miss Bradford shot her a sour look and then turned to the major, eyes fluttering. "I adore walking in country gardens. I would welcome some fresh air as well, Major. Would you object to my joining you?"

Mrs. Bradford, whose plump cheeks bulged with a mouth full of ham, ceased to chew and frowned at her daughter's bold question. When Myra ignored her stare, the mother turned a porcine glare of disapproval on the major.

"Pray, forgive me, Miss Bradford, but I have a matter of some import about which I wished to speak with Miss Fields. We shall require some privacy." Roderick knew he was being excessively rude to the London beauty, but he wouldn't let Elizabeth escape his wrath. He'd spent a long and uncomfortable night in his sister's room. He fully intended to vent his anger on the lady responsible while all his aches and pains reminded him of her prank.

Her innocent greeting this morning had nearly caused him to doubt his conclusions. But she'd shown not the least remorse when inquiring about his sister's absence from the breakfast parlour. Hearing Imogene's name on the lady's lips had strengthened his resolve to unmask her plot. Elizabeth was aptly suited for the stage.

Sir Gordon, seeing an opportunity to ingratiate himself with Miss Bradford, spoke into the silence which greeted the major's refusal. "My dear, allow me to take you down the Border Walk to the river. 'Tis quite a sight to behold with the morning sun sparkling on the water."

"I should be delighted, sir," the lady simpered, giving Elizabeth a smug look.

Mrs. Bradford returned to her meal, relieved that her ungrateful child would not be with the major. She would never understand Myra's fascination with the penniless army officer. Sir Gordon might do as a distraction for now, but with the Langley fortune her daughter could look as high as a duke for a husband. The plump lady speared another slice of the ham and relished the thought of no longer living in rooms in Cheapside.

Miss Langley, quietly observing the major, chuckled softly while feeding bacon to Reynard. Her house party was turning out to be far more amusing than even she'd imagined. 'Twas a shame she had to pick an inheritor, for she liked the company and would regret seeing them leave.

"I must get a bonnet, sir," Elizabeth said. "I shall join you in the Great Hall in ten minutes."

The major, having courteously risen when she stood, agreed to the plan.

Hurrying to her room, Elizabeth found her chip-straw bonnet with the yellow flowers that matched her dress. Tying the ribbon into a bow, she took one last appraising glance in the mirror at her gown. The pale yellow bodice with puffed sleeves covered a white muslin inset which formed a flattering ruffle about her neck. The muslin skirt was white with matching yellow dots.

Pleased with her appearance, Elizabeth donned a pair of lace gloves and made her way down to the hall where the major awaited. Despite his rather grim appearance, she thought him stunningly handsome in his red tunic with cream-trimmed lapels. She wondered if his wounded limb might be bothering him.

Roderick watched Miss Fields come down the stairs towards him. He swore he would not be swayed by her beauty, but he felt a masculine response stirring deep within him when she placed a gloved hand upon the arm he extended to her.

Elizabeth covered her nerves with a rush of banalities about the weather. They exited the Hall and crossed the moat walking deep into the decorative topiary.

The major led her down the Statue Walk of which she'd heard, but he showed no inclination to stop and admire the stone figures. Instead, he gave only clipped responses to her comments, otherwise he remained silent. Finally they came to worn flagstones which lay beside a great yew hedge that was neatly trimmed. At an opening in the shrubbery, they entered into the Enclosed Garden.

A gardener working on the roses stopped and tugged a battered felt hat from his head. The major acknowledged the man with a slight nod, and the servant replaced his hat, returning to his work.

"Why, sir, this is beautiful. I shall have to bring Julia here, for she so enjoys secluded spots for reading." Elizabeth dropped her hand from the major's arm as she admired the hedge-bordered garden. A gravel path cut an oval walk through the roses and other flowers, ending at a small summerhouse at the opposite side of the enclosure.

Roderick watched Elizabeth walk down the path away from him. She stopped and exchanged a few words with the old gardener, then continued towards the rear of the garden. He would allow her to finish her raptures about the Enclosed Garden, for he wasn't certain he could keep his temper under control just yet.

Following behind the lady, he was startled when the busy gardener suddenly stopped and handed him a red rose. "For your lady, sir."

Why, the old man thought they were paramours. At the moment, he was far more likely to strangle her than kiss her. About to return the flower to the presumptuous servant, he was stayed by the kindness in the fellow's eyes. There was no reason to embarrass the old man for his mistaken assumption. Roderick merely thanked the gardener, then followed Miss Fields to the opposite side of the garden, uncertain what to do with the crimson bloom.

Elizabeth took a seat on a marble bench a ways in front of the summerhouse to enjoy the warmth of the morning sun. She looked up to see the major walking towards her. Observing the lovely flower he held, she felt a tremor of excitement rush through her. Had he asked the gardener for the rose to give to her? A smile came unbidden to her lips even as she tried to remind herself she could not fall in love for her sisters' sake.

Roderick came to a halt in front of the lady. Brusquely he thrust the flower towards her. "I believe the gardener wished you to have this."

Elizabeth took the rose, suppressing her disappointment at the source of her gift. " 'Tis very beautiful." She waved at the old man who'd ceased his work to watch the pair. Tugging his hat in reply, he gathered his basket and shears, leaving the couple to their privacy.

"Miss Fields, I demand an explanation for your conduct last night."

Startled at the major's surly tone, Elizabeth looked up to see an angry glint in his green eyes. "What can you mean, sir?"

"Don't take me for a fool. Did you think I could not guess who came to frighten my sister by simple elimination of those who had the opportunity and the audacity to enact such a prank?"

"Someone frightened your sister?" Elizabeth was baffled, but even as she asked the question, realization dawned that the major, instead of harboring tender emotions for her, was accusing her of deliberately trying to terrorize a young girl. "You think I did such a despicable thing?"

The show of innocence on the lady's face only helped to enrage Roderick. There could have been no other responsible. "I saw you with my own eyes prancing about Imogene's bedchamber with some kind of material over your head to make you look like a ghost—and with little regard to my sister's sensibilities."

Shaking her head in denial, Elizabeth could only say, "Major Shelton, I do assure you I did not—"

"Would you have me believe it was Miss Powers or Miss Hartman? I know that everyone else was in playing cards for it was just past eleven."

"Sir, I would not play such a prank on—"

"Oh, but you would, Miss Fields. Your own friend, Miss Powers, told me that you were notorious in your parish for every imaginable kind of escapade." The major noted two angry red stains had appeared on the lady's cheeks.

Slanting her chin upwards, Elizabeth hotly retorted, "There are few people, Major, who have led exemplary lives. I have much to regret about my youthful antics, but I am telling you that I did not come to your sister's room last night dressed as myself *or* as a ghost."

Roderick dragged his gaze from the lady's angry face. Her tone was so convincing, yet he knew that the intruder was a woman. Could he be wrong? As the face of the timid Miss Powers and the prim and proper Miss Hartman flashed in his mind, he was certain neither would have the courage or deviousness for such a daring prank. "As a soldier, I have learned to trust my instincts, Miss Fields. I know what I saw last night, and I saw a woman masquerading as a ghost." He turned to give her a cold stare. "I am certain it was you."

Elizabeth's fingers tightened on the rose, causing a thorn to prick her through her gloves, but her anger was so great she paid scant notice to the tingle of pain. "And pray, what was the purpose of my cavorting about your sister's room as a spirit, Major?"

"To frighten her away from Langley Hall and eliminate her from consideration for the legacy. I can assure you that your playing at being a ghost shall not work, for I am here to protect Imogene from your schemes." Roderick frowned down at the young woman whose beauty still managed to awe him even as he berated her.

Consumed by rage at the false accusation and the manner in which it had been issued, Elizabeth affixed him with a cold, hard glare as she rose from the bench with dignity. "Major Shelton, if I were a man, I would challenge you to a duel for this slander. Since I cannot, I can only hope this so-called ghost you *claim* to have seen is genuine and that it haunts you every night while you remain at Langley Hall."

"Claim! Madam, I don't lie."

"Nor do I, Major." Tossing the rose to the ground, Elizabeth angrily stalked back to the Hall, leaving the major behind in the Enclosed Garden in an equally bad temper.


Julia glanced up from her book at the sound of a slamming door when Elizabeth entered the Orangery. The lady angrily tugged the straw bonnet from her head, leaving her brown curls tousled.

A sudden feeling of dismay filled Julia at the look on her friend's usually gentle features. She had not seen Elizabeth so outraged since Squire Brimley's son tried to steal a kiss when she was but fifteen.

"What has sent you into the boughs, Lizzie?"

"The nerve of that man to accuse me of such an outrageous trick. I am so angry I don't think I shall be able to be civil when I meet him again. 'Tis beyond thinking about." Elizabeth stalked to the bench where Julia sat, but her agitation was so great she continued to pace about in front of her friend.

"Sir Gordon?"

"That fop!" She threw up her hand in dismissal. "Heavens, no, I was referring to Major Shelton."

Julia had a sinking sensation in her stomach. Her hopes had been high when the major had invited Elizabeth for a walk after breakfast. What had happened to the budding romance she'd detected? "What has he done to overset you?"

"That arrogant bully accused me of dressing myself as a ghost and trying to frighten his sister into leaving the Hall. As if I would do such a foolish thing."

Julia arched one eyebrow at her friend, saying nothing.

With a huff, Elizabeth admitted, "All right, I might have done such a thing when younger, but I would never have played such a prank on Imogene for I quite like her. I can only pity the poor child for having a tyrannical brother like the major."

"Yes, I am sure it is a great trial having a dashingly handsome brother who protects and loves her." Quietly observing her outraged friend, Julia realized that much of Elizabeth's anger was that a man she'd much admired had made the accusation. "You are too angry to think rationally at present, my dear. Give yourself some time, for I am sure that tempers flared. Once you and the major are more yourselves you can calmly explain to him that it was not you. I am sure as soon as his own ire cools he will listen."

Elizabeth, passing a pot of daisies growing on a pedestal, snatched a single flower from the pot. The lovely bloom soon fell victim to her distress, its petals plucked one by one and dropped under the lady's pacing slippers. With a wicked chuckle, she suggested, "I am so annoyed I could push him into the moat. That would cool his anger quickly enough."

Alarmed that her friend might do just that in the heat of her emotions, Julia knew she needed to do something. "Why not go for a good gallop? It will clear your thoughts."

Elizabeth nodded in agreement, for she knew she'd never do something so childish, despite her jest. But no ride could ease the wound in her heart. "Will you join me?"

"No. I could not keep apace with you in your present mood. Go and dash about on that sweet mare you rode the other day. I am certain you will be feeling more the thing when you return." Julia rose and kissed her friend on the cheek.

As Elizabeth turned to leave, Julia asked, "Just one thing, when did this ghost appear to Miss Shelton?"

Distractedly Elizabeth pushed back the disheveled curls from her face. "I believe the major said just before midnight. That was why he was so certain I was the culprit, for the others were still playing cards."

"I see. Well, don't give it another thought for now. Simply enjoy your ride."

"I shall try."

Elizabeth exited the glassed terrace, but without her usual enthusiasm. This would not do, Julia thought. Regardless of her friend's ranting about the major, she was certain Elizabeth was smitten with the handsome soldier. She'd never shown so much partiality for any other gentleman of her acquaintance.

Julia sat for a long time in thought, reminded of her own disappointments in love. Then she rose, walked to the glass, and looked out over the manicured lawn which stretched to the moat and beyond. Her own situation might still be hopeless, but how could she convince the major he was wrong, that her friend hadn't played the ghost? She reviewed Lizzie's actions the previous evening during the time of the midnight visitation. With dawning realization, Julia knew she had proof that Elizabeth couldn't have enacted the ghost.

Hurriedly she left the Orangery to search out the major. She entered the Great Hall just as Sir Gordon and Miss Bradford returned from their outing by the river.

Miss Bradford smirked at Julia as she removed a large straw bonnet decorated with clusters of waxed purple grapes. "It would seem that Miss Fields and the major have argued. He was quite alone just now. His face was so grim that Sir Gordon and I hesitated to speak to him. But one must remember the proprieties, and we greeted him properly as we passed. Why, he was barely civil in return. Just a nod of his head, then he stormed his way to the riverbank."

Julia shrugged as if the matter were of no importance to her, but she was eager to be on her way now that she knew where the soldier was. "A mere misunderstanding, no doubt easily set to rights after Elizabeth returns from her ride. Pray excuse me."

Sir Gordon watched Miss Powers hurry up the stairs. Was something afoot which he might take advantage of? he wondered. It might be prudent for him to keep his eyes open. Seeing the doors to the Queen's Drawing Room, a plan formed in his mind. The chamber was perfectly situated to watch the comings and goings of the major and the others, if one left the doors open.

"Miss Bradford, I cannot tell you how much I enjoyed our walk." The baronet gave his most winning grin, even as he allowed his eyes to drift to the twin mounds of flesh exposed by the buxom lady's fashionable morning gown. A tasty morsel, he thought. Perhaps he should encourage Cousin Esmé to choose the London beauty. "We have so much in common, unlike the others. They are so sadly unaware of the joys of Society. 'Tis such a delight to spend the morning with a lady like yourself—beautiful and interested in the latest *on dits*. Might I beg a few more minutes of your company? Allow me to show you the Queen's Drawing Room."

Myra fluttered her lashes just the way her mama had shown her and smiled up at Sir Gordon. How fashionably elegant he appeared. And why had she never noticed before just how handsome he was? Because she'd been distracted by the major in his regimental jacket. Well, no

more. Here was a gentleman who admired her. "I should
be delighted, Sir Gordon."

The baronet led her across the Great Hall. Gesturing
the footman away, he opened the double doors and ushered her into a rather drab room decorated with dark
green silk wallpaper and drapes. Leaving the doors open
so he might see who passed, he led Miss Bradford to a
chair beside one of the two sets of windows. Even as the
lady took her seat, he peered through the glass to see if
he could catch sight of the major.

Myra looked around the room, rather disappointed in
the sedate decor. "Why is it called the Queen's Drawing
Room, sir? You must own it is rather plain for such a
regal name?"

"The chamber was originally called the Green Drawing
Room, I believe, but it was renamed by Cousin Esmé's
mother after Queen Charlotte and the princesses stopped
to have tea with the Langleys when they took a rare journey north with the king. Her majesty even brought her
favorite pug on the visit. 'Twas long before the old King
went mad."

Sir Gordon related the facts he'd heard during an earlier visit, but never took his eyes from the window. He
could barely see the River Nidd between the two great
yew hedges that created the Border Walk. Of the major
there was not a glimpse.

"I don't believe I have ever seen our poor queen. Was
she considered beautiful?"

Remembering himself, Sir Gordon said, "My dear, your
beauty has overwhelmed me to such a degree that I can
only say, no lady in the land could rival you."

Myra tittered with delight. "Sir Gordon, you are too
kind."

In an extravagant gesture, he went down on one knee
before her chair, arms extended. "Sweet lady, I would

beg the gods to allow me to kneel at your feet to worship your beauty for a lifetime."

"Oh, Sir Gordon." Myra was breathless at the flattery. She'd never had a beau so smitten before. She dropped her gaze shyly to the floor as her mama had tutored her to do in just this sort of situation. It would never do to appear too eager. Even if she didn't get the legacy, here was a gentleman who could fulfill her dearest wish—to be truly a part of Polite Society in fact and not in fabrication.

At the sound of footsteps on the stairs, Sir Gordon peered around the chair. Miss Powers, dressed for the outdoors, fairly flew past the open door. Very likely she was on her way to convince the major to go after Miss Fields and apologize for whatever misunderstanding they'd had.

Sir Gordon stood up abruptly, causing Miss Bradford to start. He must get to Ryland. If the interfering spinster and the soldier reconciled, they would cheerfully return to cause more trouble for him. His ingenious valet might think of something to prevent the happy reconciliation.

"Is something wrong, sir?"

"Pray excuse me, dear lady. I have just remembered the most urgent matter."

Sir Gordon rushed from the room.

"But I thought . . ." Watching the baronet disappear up the stairs, Myra finished the sentence dejectedly, ". . . that you wished to worship at my feet for a lifetime."

# *Eight*

Julia tied the ribbon to her bonnet as she dashed out the door in her quest to find the major. She crossed the moat and strode briskly to the Border Walk. Entering the plant-lined corridor, she paid little heed to the blue delphiniums, yellow Achillea, or purple mallows nestled against the large bordering yew hedges. Her only interest was in finding Major Shelton.

Hurrying down the path, she could see the sparkle of the river at the end of the long walk. Minutes later she ran the soldier to ground some ways up the rock-lined stream.

Roderick, troubled by his encounter with Elizabeth, had continued to walk, attempting to justify his behavior in the Enclosed Garden. Had he been wrong about her? The outraged look on the lady's face as she'd tried to defend herself ripped at his confidence. Pondering the accuracy of his accusations, he looked up to see Miss Powers coming along the riverbank towards him, an intent look upon her face.

"Major Shelton, I have been searching for you."

"Good day, Miss Powers. Have you come to cut out my tongue for accusing Miss Fields of infamous conduct?" Guilt and doubt about the scene in the Enclosed Garden caused him to make light of the matter.

"I have not, but I warn you to beware of Lizzie. She is

very handy with a blade, for her eldest brother taught her to fence." Julia spoke in a teasing tone, for nothing got one's back up more than being told they'd made a mistake.

"Miss Fields has spent a lifetime engaged in unconventional behavior, yet she is outraged that I accuse her of such." Roderick shook his head in puzzlement and looked out over the water.

"Knowing Lizzie these many years, I can assure you that she might very likely have conceived such a plot, but never against an innocent like your sister. Besides, I have reason to know she is blameless for this particular trick, since she arrived in my rooms before eleven last evening and did not leave until well past midnight." Julia didn't mention that much of their conversation had centered on this man while her friend attempted to explain away her fascination.

"Are you certain it was not Miss Fields under that sheet, or do you merely wish to protect a much beloved friend?" Roderick's stomach tightened into a knot as he realized the extent of his mistake, for even as he questioned Miss Powers, he knew her to be a lady of integrity.

"I am certain Elizabeth Fields was not your ghost." The lady gazed at him with compassion on her face.

"Then I made a dreadful mistake." Roderick turned his back on Miss Powers and walked to the edge of the river, while the full import of his crime weighed on him. But even as he regretted his rash attack on Miss Fields, the question of who did make the nocturnal visit to his sister demanded an answer.

He looked back at Miss Powers ruefully. "I hope you understand how I came to make such a grievous error, for I am certain that the 'ghost' was a woman. Besides Miss Fields, there was only yourself and Miss Hartman to consider. Can you not see how your friend was the likeliest candidate?"

Julia laughed and nodded her head. Growing quiet, she pondered the possibilities. "There is someone else who might have played the ghost, a woman you have not considered."

Roderick looked a question at the lady.

"My abigail informed me that there is something of a romance between Sir Gordon's valet and one of the upstairs maids. A village girl named Trudie. There is much discussion among the servants that she fairly dotes on the man and would, no doubt, do his bidding."

"Good heavens, I never considered the servants, except the valet. I dismissed him after I became certain that it was a woman beneath the linen. No doubt the maid would deny any part, should I accuse her."

"I think you have made enough accusations for one day, Major," Julia replied gently. "If it was Trudie, I am certain you gave her such a scare she shan't play the prank a second time."

Roderick thought he was past the age to blush, but he felt his neck warm at the truth of the lady's words. "You are correct. I must make my apologies to Miss Fields. Do you think she will forgive my unyielding arrogance?"

"Dear Lizzie has a kind heart. Perhaps by now her temper has cooled sufficiently to hear an apology with civility."

Taking Miss Powers's arm, Roderick began to usher her hurriedly back towards the house. He cursed his wounded leg for making him so slow. He was filled with a fire to make amends to the lady, convincing himself that it was the right thing to do and his eagerness had nothing to do with any tender emotions he might feel. "Do you know where I might find her?"

"She is riding, sir. I am certain they will be able to give you her direction at the stables, if you should choose to go after her. Knowing Lizzie, I am positive she will be gone for some time."

"Yes, that is an excellent suggestion, Miss Powers." Despite his injury, the major's pace was so rapid he drew Julia back up the Border Walk at a near run. Filled with an urge to be on Orion's back, he hoped the exercise would help him clear his mind before he faced the lady who so disturbed his thoughts.

Some ten minutes later, the major rode away from the stables at a full gallop in the direction he'd been informed Elizabeth and her accompanying groom had gone.

Shaking his head, Willet, the head groom, muttered about the Quality and their fits and starts. First Miss Fields comes out asking for her a horse, in a rare temper, and now the major, equally in a taking, wants to know about the lady.

Latching the gate on the stall where the major's horse had been, the old man looked up to see the baronet's valet marching into the stables.

"I need Sir Gordon's mount, man, and be quick about it. I am on an errand of some urgency," Ryland barked the order as he shifted a large parcel under his arm.

Willet thought the man strutted about as though his master already owned the Hall. Dislike settled in the old man's stomach like one of his late wife's puddings, heavy and sour. "I reckon one of the carriage 'orses is good enough for the likes of you."

Ryland's eyes narrowed. "You forget that Sir Gordon will likely be master here one day, and *we* shan't forget any slights."

Having Miss Langley's assurance that he'd be comfortably pensioned off at the end of the year, Willet smirked at the valet as he turned towards the rear of the stable. "Shaw, put a saddle on Majestic. He's due some exercise."

"I assume he is a suitable mount." Ryland couldn't be delayed with some obstinate sluggard.

"Fastest 'orse Miss Langley owns." Willet chortled as

he failed to mention that the stallion, a gift from the squire, was also only green broke and would very likely put the smug servant in the dirt.

"Excellent." Ryland gazed intently in the direction the major had taken.


Sir Gordon stood just inside the moat, watching the front drive. He felt a rush of nervous excitement course through his veins. Ryland was confident that he could come up with a plan to discredit Miss Fields and Major Shelton, if he could find them. That would surely put the Misses Powers and Shelton at a disadvantage with Esmé. What gently bred lady wouldn't be overset at finding a friend or relative involved in a scandal?

He'd not pressed Ryland for details of his plan, only ordered the man to get the job done. The baronet was certain his servant would not do anything to harm the pair, for the man had no wish to have his neck stretched on the gallows. But the valet had immediately said he knew what should be done to cause a stir.

Suddenly the sound of pounding hooves alerted Sir Gordon that the man was mounted and in pursuit of Miss Fields and the major. Ryland came barreling down the gravel path from the stables on a rawboned bay stallion Sir Gordon recognized as one of his cousin's. The servant struggled to control the animal as the beast dashed head-long into a large rhododendron which lined the carriage way. When the horse failed to unseat his rider, the animal crow-hopped across the drive into a low-growing holly tree, before dancing in a circle, snorting in frustration. At last managing to get the troublesome steed somewhat in hand, Ryland attempted to ride him up the front drive.

"Ryland, you fool! I told you to take my horse!" Sir Gordon shouted as he watched his servant vie with the barely trained animal.

The hapless valet made no response. He concentrated on urging the horse forward. The man knew the major was getting farther away every moment he delayed.

Sir Gordon watched the horse and rider cut a zigzag path up the drive at breakneck speed, brushing first a sculpted box hedge on the right, then one on the left. In the battle between animal and man, the animal appeared to be winning.

The bay's speed was excellent, the baronet thought, if only Ryland could get the beast under control. Then, as if the valet had heard Sir Gordon's thought, the servant managed to keep the horse on a straight path for the last twenty feet of the driveway.

The baronet sighed with relief when the animal picked up speed as horse and rider disappeared through the gates of Langley. His man had never failed him before, and Sir Gordon was certain he would not do so now.

Turning back to the Hall, he entered and inquired about the location of his cousin from the footman on duty. Informed the lady was at her accounts in the library, the baronet strode across the hall, stopping briefly at a mirror to check the condition of his blond curls. Satisfied that he looked his best, he tapped on the door and was bade to enter.

Sir Gordon stepped into the library. Esmé was seated behind a large oak desk with several ledgers opened in front of her. Behind her, on a window seat, sat Reynard, who raised his head to eye the visitor. He seemingly determined the baronet to be of little interest and laid his head back down, but continued to watch the man.

Esmé looked up from the sums she'd been totaling as her cousin entered the library. He was as fine looking a man as she'd ever had the good fortune to see. She thought the russet coat with matching cream and russet waistcoat he wore was surprisingly subdued for this flamboyant dandy. Seeing the intense look in his brown eyes, she was curious as to what new scheme he'd come up with.

Laying down her quill, she politely inquired, "What can I do for you, sir?"

"I hope you shan't think me too precipitous in coming to you this way, dear Esmé, but an admirable thought has occurred to me."

"Ah, a rare moment indeed." Esmé bit her lip to keep from smiling.

Sir Gordon frowned briefly, wondering if he'd received an insult, then pushed the thought aside. "Knowing that it is your wish to leave your estate to one of the ladies, I thought perhaps I might offer my name as protection to the lady you choose."

"You wish to marry my chosen heiress? How noble indeed!"

Sir Gordon failed to note the mockery in his cousin's tone. "Yes, I thought so myself, for you must admit that you were pursued by every gazetted fortune hunter in your day. The lady will not only receive the sanctuary of my name to keep her from such dangers, but she will be Lady Mondell, which is no small thing in Society. 'Tis the least I can do for you, Cousin."

Esmé's gaze dropped to the household accounts on her desk. As much as she hated to admit it, the man was right. By the time she was eighteen, she'd come to believe every offer of marriage was motivated by greed. The fortune hunters and gamblers had come in droves to court her over the years, but wariness had made her refuse all offers. Now here she was an old woman, never having known the joys of matrimony. Was she about to sentence one of these girls to the same fate?

But was Sir Gordon any better than the lot who'd pursued her? She looked up to see the fop eyeing her hopefully. He was young and vain, but she'd never heard that there was any true vice in him. She knew from her friends in London that he didn't game or drink to excess.

Unfortunately, she was not certain there was enough virtue in him to make a good husband. Perhaps if he were in love his nobler qualities might surface.

Coming to a quick decision, Esmé rose and picked up her cane. She walked around the desk and stood before the young man.

The small fox terrier, seeing his mistress moving, jumped up and came to stand with her in front of the baronet. The dog sniffed the man's shiny Hessians with interest.

"My dear Sir Gordon, I have no objection to your marrying one of the girls, but you must genuinely care for the lady you choose and she for you. Therefore you must make your choice before I make mine. Is that understood?"

"But, Cousin, how can I—?" Sir Gordon was flustered. This wasn't what he wanted. He wanted the heiress, not just any bride.

"Choose before I do, or I shall not endorse the marriage." So saying, Esmé started toward the door as fast as her infirmity would allow.

Sir Gordon closed his eyes, praying that Ryland accomplished his mission thereby lowering the number of candidates to one. When at last he opened them he discovered that Esmé's cursed dog had relieved himself on his new Hessians before joining his mistress.

Sir Gordon swore soundly as he hurried to his room to remove his soiled boots and to anxiously await the return of his valet.


Elizabeth reined her horse at the top of the hill, stopping to admire the Yorkshire countryside. The open field in front of her was dotted with a large flock of black-faced sheep grazing contentedly. She could see glimpses of the River Nidd through the trees as it wound its way south. The tranquility of the scene did much to calm her irritated nerves.

The sound of the groom's horse as it galloped up behind her, caused her to turn and smile at the freckle-faced man whose shock of red hair hung raggedly from beneath his battered hat.

Bringing his mount to a halt in back of her, he returned a grin. "Yer a great goer, miss. But ye can't lose me. Started out with the squire, I did, and there ain't a better rider in all England."

"Truly, I did not mean to leave you behind, Shaw. However did you come to Miss Langley's employ?" Elizabeth asked, curious about why he'd left the likable squire's estate.

"Squire keeps givin' 'er a new weanlin' every year, and Willet was complainin' about being too old to be gentlin' the animals, so I volunteered to come and do it. The blunt's good and not so many 'orses to 'andle, 'cept maybe now, what with all the extra guests."

Elizabeth nodded her head, turning back to admire the view. She had tried to push all thoughts of the scene in the garden from her mind during her ride. She just wanted to enjoy the wind on her face and the feel of the reins in her gloved hands. But now that she'd stopped, all her anger at the major's accusations came rushing back. The man had been insufferable.

A loud bleating startled her out of her bitter thoughts, and Elizabeth spied a young lamb who'd become separated from its mother. She felt sorry for the little one as it dashed about among the grazing animals frantically calling out. At last a large ewe some distance away raised her head and gave a loud *baa*. The lamb scampered to its mother's side, contentedly nuzzling her white fleece.

Elizabeth smiled at the scene. Even in the animal kingdom familial ties were important. The lamb once again feeling secure began to frolic about its mother.

The bond with her own family was the most meaningful thing in her life. Could she really blame Major Shelton for so strongly defending Imogene? Elizabeth knew she might well have assailed any person who played such a prank on Ruth or Sarah.

With a mirthless laugh, she realized she didn't blame the major for his defense of his sister. She blamed him for accusing her of being the culprit. Knowing she hadn't played the ghost, she suddenly wondered who had.

The groom interrupted her thoughts. "Miss, I think ye've got someone comin' to join ye."

Elizabeth glanced in the direction in which the man was pointing. Her back straightened with indignation when she spied flashes of Major Shelton's maroon riding coat through the trees as he cantered along the road below. How dare he come to rail at her again?

Anger surged in her. She would not sit here and meekly wait for him to come and hurl new accusations. "Shaw, I shall not need you to ride with me now that the major has come. You may return to the stables."

The groom looked doubtful, knowing it was strictly proper for him to remain. "Are ye certain, miss? I don't mind ridin' with ye and the major."

Anxious to be rid of the man, she smiled politely. "I am certain you have many duties to attend to, and we might be out here riding for hours. You needn't worry about me now that Major Shelton is here."

Elizabeth was certain she could evade the pursuing soldier by herself, but with Shaw tagging along behind her it would be impossible.

The groom tugged obediently at his hat, then turned his horse back towards the Hall. He didn't like leaving the lady, but what was a servant to do? He guided his animal in the direction of the major.

Some minutes later, as the two men rode past one another, Shaw called, "Miss Fields is restin' on the rise, sir."

"Thank you." Roderick looked up through the trees. He saw Elizabeth gazing down at him, then suddenly she spun her horse around and disappeared over the hill. He surmised that the lady was still very angry with him. He couldn't blame her, but he was determined to issue an apology. With a gentle nudge of his heel, he urged Orion into a full gallop.

By the time he got to the crest of the hill, Elizabeth was just disappearing into a line of trees on the far side of the meadow. His heart practically stopped when she entered a narrow, overgrown path in the woods at a full gallop. The foolish woman might break her neck just to avoid another encounter with him.

Orion's stride lengthened on the open ground and within minutes Roderick entered the woods at full speed. He occasionally caught glimpses of the white scarf which trailed from the lady's hat or a flash of blue from her riding habit. Urging his horse faster, he closed the gap. As the trail straightened, he saw Elizabeth gallop towards a fallen tree that blocked the path.

He held his breath as the lady bore down on the huge old oak. Even he would hesitate to put a trustworthy animal like Orion over such a large obstacle. As her grey horse sailed into the air, he involuntarily shouted, "Miss Fields!"

Elizabeth thought she heard someone shouting, but her heart was pounding so loudly in her ears as Luna tucked her long legs and jumped the fallen tree, she dismissed it as imagination. The fleet little mare performed beautifully over the highest jump Elizabeth had ever made. But as the animal landed on the far side of the tree, she lost her footing for a moment, then righted herself before continuing down the narrow path.

What madness was this? Elizabeth knew she very likely

might hurt herself, or worse this fine horse, just because she was out of countenance with Major Shelton. Reining in, she slowed her mount to a walk to allow the plucky little goer to cool and the major to catch up. After all, she was not in the wrong here, he was.

Elizabeth followed the trail for a good distance, expecting the soldier to join her soon. At last she guided the horse into a large clearing in the trees, where another riding path intersected the one on which she rode. She stopped Luna and looked back, wondering if the major had given up the pursuit.

While sitting there, debating about whether she should return to the fallen tree to see if the major had made the attempt and failed or go on ahead, a rustling in the bushes caught her attention.

At first she could see nothing, then movement under a small elm tree caught her eye. There, nestled in among a cluster of wild bluebells lay a large brown hare, one of its legs between the jaws of a poacher's trap.

Filled with horror at the sight, Elizabeth slid down from her horse and ran to help the defenseless creature. Her sudden approach only frightened the hare more, causing it to thrash about wildly, trying to escape her.

Backing away some distance, she began to croon softly to the animal as she removed her hat, tossing it heedlessly to the ground. Looking at the trap, she wondered if she would be strong enough to help the animal. "Calm down little fellow. I shall get you out of there."

Just then she caught a glimpse of the major as he slowly trotted through the wood towards the clearing. Forgetting her grievance against him, she dashed to the opening of the path. "Major Shelton, come quickly! I need your assistance!"

Roderick looked up to see Miss Fields standing on the trail ahead of him. Her horse stood some ways behind her in a small clearing with reins dragging on the ground.

Her hat was gone, and strands of brown curls were loose about her beautiful face. Thinking she'd taken a bad spill, his hands clenched into tight fists on the reins as he spurred Orion into a canter.

He dismounted the moving horse, allowing the animal to run free into the opening as he grasped Elizabeth shoulder. "How are you hurt?"

"Me? Not in the least, I found—"

Roderick's hands dropped away from the lady as anger replaced the relief he'd felt on hearing she was unharmed. "You may have no regard for your own safety, Miss Fields, but it is unconscionable that you would endanger Miss Langley's horse in such a manner with that mad ride through these woods."

"Oh, fiddle-faddle, sir, I am not one of your soldiers to be reprimanded. There is a hare caught in a poacher's trap, and I need help getting him out, not a jaw-me-dead for my behavior."

Elizabeth ignored the startled look on the major's face and returned to where the animal was still thrashing about in the underbrush. The major came and stood beside her. Looking up at him she could see the clenching and unclenching of his jaw. She knew he was very angry with her, but now was not the time for settling matters. "Do you think he can be saved?"

Roderick didn't trust himself to speak at that moment. Instead he removed his hat and bent down under the small tree. He placed a calming hand on the hare to prevent the frightened animal from doing further harm to his leg. With his other hand, he turned the trap ever so slightly back and forth, inspecting the device.

Luck had been with the hare, for a branch had been seized between the metal jaws at the same time as the animal, preventing the device from breaking its small leg.

"Hold the hare while I release the trap." Roderick

barked the order as if he'd been speaking to a new recruit.

"Yes, sir." Elizabeth made a mock salute, then bent down and gently took hold of the hare. She didn't know what demon was propelling her to antagonize the major.

Her hand brushed his as they exchanged the hold on the hare. A sudden shock tingled up her arm, leaving her feeling amazed and almost frightened that this man could effect her thus. She pushed the thought from her mind and concentrated on the soft feel of the hare's fur. Seeing the terrified look in the animal's eyes, she turned her full attention to her task. "There, there, fellow. Don't be frightened."

The major applied pressure to the release spring, and the steel jaws relaxed. The second the hare was free of the trap he darted out of Elizabeth's hold and disappeared into the woods.

Elizabeth rose and brushed the leaves from her riding habit as the major reclosed the trap so as to prevent any other animals from becoming ensnared. As the soldier rose to face her, she eyed him warily. She didn't want to think about the pleasurable feel of their hands touching, instead she decided he deserved an apology for her pertness and thanks for aiding her with the hare. "Major Shelton, I do humbly beg—"

Roderick raised a hand to silence her. "Miss Field, in my worry for your safety I forgot myself. I had no right to reprimand you. The reason I came was to speak with you. I owe you an apology for the grievous accusations I made this morning. Miss Powers informed me that you could not have played the ghost since you were in her apartments at the time."

Elizabeth was peeved that he'd taken Julia's word when he'd ignored her own avowals of innocence. About to issue a stinging retort, she was stunned into silence when both horses, which had been standing quietly on the opposite side of the clearing, suddenly reared and then bolted into the woods.

"What the devil?" Roderick walked to the middle of the clearing. He stood staring up the path down which the horses had disappeared, troubled by the strange occurrence.

Elizabeth came to stand beside him. "Good heavens, sir! We are stranded and miles from the Hall."

"Yes, we are Miss Fields, thanks to your foolish dash through these woods."

"I don't remember inviting you to join me, sir. You are the one who chose to come. No doubt you intend to blame me for frightening the horses as well? Perhaps it was your 'ghost' come to prove her existence." Elizabeth angrily turned her back on the gentleman.

Before Roderick could give a retort, a figure dressed in a long homespun black cloak stepped into the clearing. Strangely, the cape was covered with large clumps of dirt. The man's face was masked with a black knit cloth with small eyeholes. Aiding in the disguise was a large brimmed hat pulled low over his face. A green twig clung to the top of the hat, as if he'd bumped into a tree on his way through the woods.

As Roderick's gaze fell to the dueling pistol aimed directly at them, he heard Elizabeth's soft gasp. Instinctively he stepped between the lady and the villain.

The blackguard growled in a muffled coarse voice, "Don't take another step or I'll blow a 'ole in ye, soldier."

# Nine

Fear raced through Elizabeth when she looked back at the soldier only to see a cloaked stranger with a weapon pointed at them. As Major Shelton stepped protectively in front of her, a strong urge to cling to his arm rushed through her.

Standing on her toes to get close to the major's ear, she whispered, "Is he a highwayman?"

The major shook his head as he softly answered, "I don't know."

The brigand shook the gun. "Stubble it afore I put a hole in ye."

An eerie silence fell in the clearing, then the sound of a wood wren's cheerful chirping echoed through the trees, an odd counterpoint of normalcy in this strange happening. Elizabeth's curiosity overcame her fear, and she peeked around the major.

The stranger's dark gaze darted around the clearing as if he expected to be apprehended at any minute. Apparently satisfied that they were alone, he seemed to come to a decision and growled, " 'Appen, soldier, ye best start leading the lady up this 'ere path." He gestured to the trail down which the horses had fled.

Roderick cursed his lack of a weapon. Keeping Elizabeth away from the brigand, he edged her around the armed man. Urging her up the path with a nod of his head, the major was determined to keep her out of the line of fire.

He was puzzled. This was clearly not some ordinary robbery. "What do you want? Let Miss Fields go, she has nothing of value to be taken."

"Can't do that, soldier. Need the both of ye together, I do. Now, stop yer gabblin' and get movin'."

Roderick fell silent. What could this brigand want with them both? His gaze trailed over Elizabeth's trim back as he followed her up the path. He knew she was frightened, it was only natural. He wished he could reassure her that all would be well, but he wasn't certain that would be the truth.

As she trudged over the uneven ground, he admired the way she'd refrained from hysterics and marched along with her head high and her pace brisk. Whatever else he thought of Miss Fields, he knew she had more mettle than many men.

The little-used path was nearly overgrown in places, slowing their progress. The occasional scurrying of an animal along the ground or the sudden fluttering of a grouse frightened out of the bushes were the only sounds to disturb the quiet of the forest.

As she led the way, Elizabeth's fear grew, though she followed their captor's gruff commands. Hearing the crunch of gravel beneath the major's boots reassured her, for she was not alone in this desperate situation. He would certainly try to protect them, but from what? They were in a remote part of Miss Langley's estate and being held at gunpoint by . . . a highwayman? Or was he a footpad? Maybe just a madman. She shuddered at the thought.

The summer sun grew hot, and the path seemed to lead nowhere. Elizabeth's legs began to feel made of stone as fatigue set in, causing her steps to lag. She tugged open the collar of her riding habit, longing for a cool drink of water. She wondered what had become of Luna and the major's mount. Hopefully, the horses would make it safely back to the stables and alert Shaw that there was trouble.

"Pick up yer pace, lady," the masked man growled.

Fear renewed her strength to keep going. What did this odd man want with them? She glanced back at the major, but his handsome face gave no clue to his thoughts.

Despite the appearance of acceptance of their situation, Roderick's thoughts were in search of a means to get Elizabeth away unharmed. At present, they were at the mercy of the man in the disguise. The question was, where was he taking them?

They'd walked several miles before Roderick spied the burned thatch of an old cottage's roof. The neglected structure sat on the edge of a meadow dotted with yellow dandelions and blue cornflowers. As they drew closer, he could see that the building had suffered some disaster. The door was missing and the shutters hung ajar. Weeds choked the rosebushes beside the entryway.

As they entered the field in front of the cottage, Roderick paid scant attention to the scenic splendor, his thoughts were on getting the pistol. Could he disarm this brigand without getting himself shot or, worse, Miss Fields? The thought of her lying wounded horrified him, causing him to discard the idea.

The masked man shouted, "Go to the cottage, wench."

The major halted abruptly. He didn't like the ominous sound of their destination. Facing his captor, he demanded, "We have no intention of going into some abandoned old hut until we know what this is all about."

The man in black raised the dueling pistol. He cocked the weapon. "I'm told this 'ere's got a 'air-trigger, soldier. I don't rightly want to let daylight into ye, but they don't want to see ye back at the 'all tonight. I reckon a ball in the shoulder would be as good a way as any to keep you 'ere. I was thinkin' of just lockin' ye in the cellar if ye do as ye're told."

Behind him, Elizabeth called, "Will you promise not to harm us if we obey?"

"Aye, miss, don't want to lay no one in the dust, but I got me orders about the pair of ye."

"From whom?" Roderick demanded even as he again measured his chances of taking the man from this distance. He might risk it, but if he failed Miss Fields would be left to defend herself. He wouldn't take such a chance.

The man chuckled. "Not likely to gabble about that, soldier, or I won't get me ready. Move it!"

Seeing nothing to do but obey orders, Roderick followed Elizabeth into the partially burned cottage. There was still a strong smell of charred wood in the roofless room. The abandoned building held only pieces of broken furniture, bleached and weathered by exposure. The small portion of thatched roof that remained sagged precariously over a large room filled with spiderwebs and clusters of straw.

Surprisingly, there was a stone floor, unusual for a crofter's cottage. The layers of dead leaves and tree limbs lying about told Roderick it had been some time since the place had been occupied.

Their captor tramped in behind them, then pointed the pistol at an overturned table missing a fourth leg. "Soldier, push that scrap of furniture aside."

Roderick did as the man ordered and discovered a trapdoor in the stone floor. He slid back the bolt without being told and pulled open the portal. Musty, dank air rushed out at him. Looking back at the man, Roderick argued, "Don't make Miss Fields go down into this hole. She would suffer—"

"Put a damper on it, soldier." The man pulled a small black bag from beneath his cloak and tossed it to the major. "Ye afeard she'll run into Old Nick down there?"

The man guffawed. Then he gestured with the gun for the lady to go down the stairs. "Move, miss."

As Elizabeth stepped forward, Roderick pulled open the small pouch and discovered candles and a small tinder box. "Let me go first." Pulling one of the candles from the bag, he quickly lit the wick. He tucked the bag under his arm and looked at her. "Take heart, Miss Fields. Follow me."

The major stooped a bit as he descended into the cellar, pushing thin sheets of cobwebs from his path. The underground chamber was surprisingly large but had only two wooden benches pushed against opposite walls. Its dirt floor looked moldy and damp.

Roderick knew their predicament could have been worse, but not much, for they would have no food or water. He turned and took Miss Fields's hand as she made her way down the stairs. A need to take her in his arms to reassure her came upon him as he noted her wide eyes staring into the dark, but he suppressed the urge, for he was certain she wouldn't welcome the gesture.

The lady's boots had barely touched the dirt floor when the door above slammed shut, leaving them staring at one another in the flickering light of the lone candle. The sound of the bolt sliding home sent a chill through Roderick at the finality of their situation.

Julia stood at the window in the Yellow Saloon gazing out at the fading light. She could no longer see the blue-tinged hills in the distance as the sun sank from sight. Stars began to dot the darkening sky even as she resisted the urge to cry.

She was filled with fear and guilt. There was no one to blame but herself, for she was the one who'd sent Elizabeth to ride, then encouraged the major to go after her.

What had happened to them? The question kept swirling in her mind as the minutes ticked past.

Drawing her gaze from the view to Imogene, who sat in the window seat staring out into the darkness, Julia reached out a hand to comfort the young girl. No doubt she suffered in a different way, for her only brother was missing. "I am certain they will be found and quite safe."

"As am I. Roderick very likely has come to no harm, for he has a soldier's skill to take care of himself. 'Tis dear Elizabeth I worry about. But she seemed a good rider."

"The very best." But Julia knew that even excellent riders could have accidents. The thought sent a shiver of fear down her spine.

Behind them, the rest of the house party was assembled, with the exception of Sir Gordon, but there was no idle conversation this night. All awaited word of the search that had begun over two hours ago when Julia had learned from Imogene that her brother hadn't returned. They'd immediately gone to Cousin Esmé with their worries about their missing friend and relative. The head groom, quickly summoned, confirmed that the pair had gone out during the morning and said he hadn't seen or heard from them after Shaw returned to say they were together.

Esmé had immediately ordered all the grooms and footmen to begin a search. Sir Gordon graciously volunteered to assist. But the Langley estate was a vast property, and all knew it might be morning before they heard any news if there had been an accident.

Mrs. Bradford sat beside her daughter, looking at the latest copy of *La Belle Assemblée*. She glanced up at the ormolu clock on the mantel and gave a great sigh. She was very hungry and it was getting late, without the least hope of a tidbit to tide them over until they ate.

Still, the situation had its bright spots. While she didn't

wish anything bad on the missing pair, she knew that this
distraction could only help Myra. Eyeing the pair at the
window, she could muster little sympathy. She was glad
the major was with Miss Fields and not her daughter, for
that would have been a disaster for her plans.

Thinking of the tasty capons she'd seen roasting in the
kitchen earlier, she offered, "Do you think we ought to
go and change for dinner? 'Tis getting very late and we
cannot miss . . ." Her voice trailed off as everyone in the
room looked shocked that she could think of eating at
such a time.

At that moment Aegis entered the room, followed by
the head groom and Sir Gordon. The old man roared,
"The men have clues, madam."

"News, you fool!" Sir Gordon snapped at the nearly
deaf butler.

Esmé scanned the men's faces, but one could glean no
comfort from their expressions. "They are not found?"

Sir Gordon hung back, not certain he could keep the
joy from his voice. Ryland had outdone himself and
would be rewarded as soon as there were funds for doing
so.

Willet stepped before his mistress quietly crushing his
hat between two large callused hands. Finally the old man
spoke. "Miss Langley, we found their 'orses tied up behind the Golden Pheasant in the village, but there
weren't no sign of the major or the miss."

"Did you inquire if the innkeeper had seen either Miss
Fields or Major Shelton?" Relief flooded Esmé, for she
was certain that the pair couldn't have been injured if
the horses were safely tied at the local village inn.

"Aye, ma'am. Old Bartow says 'e didn't see 'em, but
the thin' is the smithy said a fancy rig was seen in the
village this afternoon. The jarvey handling the ribbons
told 'em the carriage was 'ired at Ripley, but didn't say
who done it, just said 'e needed a horse reshod." The

old groom cleared his throat before he imparted the last of it. "Smithy told us 'e seen a gent and a lady step up into the coach and ride away."

Esmé frowned. "And did the blacksmith know the pair?"

The old man shook his head. "Says 'e never got a look at 'em. They was actin' strangelike. Not wantin' anyone to see their faces and all. Smithy declared it all to be very 'avey-cavey, ma'am."

"I see." Esmé wished they'd learned more, but seeing the tired lines around the old man's face she came to a decision. "You have had a hard day, Willet. You and your men should go to supper now."

As the old groom left, Miss Hartman jumped to her feet. "I warned you this would happen, Esmé."

Julia, who'd come near to hear what the men had to impart, was puzzled. "What has happened? We still don't know where Elizabeth and the major are. Do you not intend to have the men continue the search?"

Miss Hartman began to pace in agitation that her prophecy had come to past. "You delude yourself, Miss Powers, if you cannot see what has occurred."

"Miss Hartman, all that has occurred is that the horses have been found and not the people." Julia's voice rose as she lost patience with the older woman's histrionics.

" 'Tis plain to the rest of us that Major Shelton has eloped with Miss Fields." Miss Hartman halted to glare at Imogene as if she were the responsible member of the family.

Sir Gordon, vastly interested in inspecting his quizzing glass for dirt interjected, "I fear Miss Hartman is correct. There can be no other explanation for the horses being tied at the inn and the mysterious couple leaving the village but that the missing pair have eloped."

"Don't be ridiculous!" Julia quite forgot her manners at the absurd suggestion. She didn't like Sir Gordon's smug look. It reminded her of her younger brother when he'd won a point over her with their mother.

"Eloped!" Imogene added her protest to Julia's. "My brother would never do anything so unconventional. Besides, he has sworn never to marry."

"What can two innocents like yourselves know about lust, the passions of men—" Miss Hartman began.

"Prudence, that will be enough." Esmé eyed the girls before her with sympathy. Her companion and cousin appeared to be correct. "I am afraid that the evidence appears to indicate Miss Fields and the major did elope. I shall order the men to cease the search, for I don't want to waste their time or endanger their lives in the dark while looking for the couple that may not be out there. Most inconsiderate of them, I must say."

"Cousin Esmé, you don't understand. Lizzie—"

"My brother would not leave without telling—"

Each of the young ladies tried to argue with Miss Langley, but she put a hand up in a staying gesture. "I am certain we shall hear the news that they are safely wed by this time tomorrow. But I want no more discussion on the matter. I insist that you go and dress for dinner, for we shall be quite late sitting down at a table as it is."

"But you cannot—" Julia began.

"The matter is closed, and I forbid either of you ladies to risk injury to yourselves by going out tonight." Esmé stubbornly refused to listen, but in a kinder tone added, "Don't forget the Scottish border can be reached quickly. I am certain wherever they are, the major is taking excellent care of your friend. Now, we must not delay dinner any longer than necessary. Change without delay."

Julia bit her lip to prevent further protest. It would do no good to argue with her cousin, for she appeared to have made up her mind. Julia, however, was certain that Elizabeth Fields would never have eloped with the major, no matter how great her infatuation with the man. But where were they?

Imogene entwined her arm with Julia's. "Come, we must do as Cousin Esmé wishes." She led the distressed young lady out of the Yellow Saloon. Once away from the others, she looked to make certain they were alone. "Don't worry, for I am certain Miss Hartman is wrong. Roderick is the very last person who would elope."

"But don't you see, Imogene? That means they are lost somewhere on this huge estate, perhaps hurt or worse, and Cousin Esmé has called off the search." Julia's voice quivered slightly as dire possibilities rushed through her mind.

"Then we must come up with a plan to continue the search without our cousin's knowledge. We are certain to think of something in time." Imogene frowned as she saw Miss Bradford and Sir Gordon exit the Yellow Saloon, the lady giggling in a most annoying manner. "Go and dress, Julia. I shall join you in your room as soon as I change for supper, and we shall make plans."

Julia was pleased that Imogene agreed with her, and was brave enough to defy their cousin's wishes for the sake of her brother. She knew they both were risking the loss of the legacy, but her conscience wouldn't allow her to sit meekly by when Elizabeth was in danger.

Roderick pushed his shoulder against the locked cellar door, but with his wounded leg and the steep slant of the stairs, he could not apply enough pressure to budge the portal in the least. He slumped on the cold stone step, looking at Miss Fields who was seated on a bench on the opposite side of the cellar. She sat quietly clutching a single candle as she watched his progress.

"I am unable to break through this cursed door."

"Don't worry, Major. I am certain our 'knight of the road' shall not return."

Roderick came down the stairs to stand in front of the lady. The soft candlelight only enhanced her beauty. "How can you be so certain? Besides, that was no highwayman, Miss Fields."

"True, for he did not rob us. As to why I am certain, I cannot explain, only that I am, sir. I don't believe we shall see that fellow again." Elizabeth smiled tentatively at the major.

That smile sent a wave of sensations through Roderick that he could ill afford to experience. Turning, he began to pace the dirt floor to remove the lady from his line of sight. "If you are so intuitive, perhaps I should recommend you to my commander, General Beresford. I am certain he would appreciate knowing what the French troops are planning in advance."

Elizabeth laughed, feeling some of the tension flow from her. "I don't profess to know the future. For I cannot tell you how long we shall be stranded here, which is certainly a fact I should like to know." She watched the soldier limp back and forth, his head bent in thought. "It might be a long wait, sir. Don't you wish to be seated? If you continue to pace a hole in the floor we shall very likely have Old Nick here with us before we are rescued. A prospect which does not please me in the least."

Roderick halted his pacing and looked at the lady. Despite her brave tone, the ordeal had taken its toll. A haunted look still rested in her lovely blue eyes as she gazed at him across the candle. He was helpless to get them out of there, but experience before going into battle had taught him that he could lessen her fears by taking her mind off their situation. With a teasing smile, he asked, "Afraid your wicked ways are about to catch up with you, Miss Fields?"

"I am certain that my friends and family would say I

should not be surprised to receive a visit from Satan. I would prefer it not to be today." Elizabeth gazed into the tiny candleflame as thoughts of her family rushed to overwhelm her. Would she ever see her brothers and sisters again? Or would she and Major Shelton die here, their bodies undiscovered for years? No, she would not think that, for she was certain Julia would not rest until they were found.

The major settled himself on the bench beside her. "You have told me but little of yourself. How many siblings do you have, Miss Fields?"

Looking up into his handsome face, Elizabeth was certain that Major Shelton had little interest in her family. He was only trying to keep her mind distracted from dark thoughts. She longed for him to take her in his arms and comfort her the way her father had when she was young and frightened of something, but the thought of such intimacy with this man sent a warming blush to her cheeks and set blood racing in her veins.

In an overwrought rush, she began to chatter to him of life at Aylsham vicarage. As she spoke, the major began to ask questions and she found herself forgetting about her dark surroundings and her fears. She was only aware of the handsome face illuminated in the golden glow and the deep resonance of his calm voice.

Roderick watched the light play on Elizabeth's face as she spoke of her siblings. Her eyes, now softened with fond memories, twinkled up at him as she told him of youthful pranks her brothers had played. He was drawn into her tales, wishing that he and Imogene had as many shared memories.

As Miss Fields told a particularly amusing tale about a sister named Ruth and a hedgehog in church, Roderick looked up and noted light no longer streamed through the crack in the trap door. Night had fallen and so had their chances of an early rescue.

* * *

"Miss Julia, I can't get your 'air up if you won't sit still," the abigail complained as her mistress fidgeted beneath her nimble fingers. The girl continued to struggle to put the finishing touches on the arrangement of curls as her mistress chattered.

"I don't give a fig about my hair, Margie. Lizzie is lost, and I am expected to go down and dine as if nothing has occurred. To suggest that she has eloped—" A knock sounded at the door, interrupting her tirade.

Julia pushed Margie's hands away and hurried to open the door herself. She was surprised to see Imogene had brought a maid with her. "Come in, my dear. I hope you have some idea about what must be done."

Imogene nodded. "This is Annie Brock, the maid who waits on Elizabeth. She heard the news and came to offer her help." The young servant curtseyed at the introduction.

"What can we do, Imogene? I shan't sit idly by while Lizzie or your brother might be lying in some ditch injured. Shall we disregard Cousin Esmé's orders and don our habits to go in search of them?"

"Miss Powers," the little maid said hesitantly, "you are more likely the one to end in a ditch if you ride about the estate at night. The countryside can be treacherous for one unfamiliar with the land. I thought my brothers might be of some 'elp."

Eagerly Julia said, "You, too, are convinced that Miss Fields did not elope!"

"Aye, Miss Powers, for the lady was cross as crabs at the major when she came to change for 'er ride. Even if they made up their differences, 'tis not likely she'd rush off that way, 'er bein' a proper brought-up young lady and all."

Imogene suddenly took note of a fact she'd not known.

"Why was Elizabeth angry with Roderick? He is forever pulling caps with me, but I have rarely heard him raise his voice to another."

"He accused Lizzie of dressing like a ghost to frighten you."

Imogene was silent for a moment. "Did she?"

"No, and so I told him, for she was with me at the time of your 'haunting.' Never mind about that. What do you suggest we do to continue the search, Annie?"

"I've got two brothers what work for Miss Langley 'erdin' sheep. I could 'ave 'em search tonight. They know the lay of the land better than anyone."

"Oh, Annie, do you think they would? I could pay them for their troubles. It would only be a small amount, for that is all I have, but do you think they can start at once?"

"I'm certain they will, miss. I'll go to our cottage and set 'em to the task."

Julia thanked the young maid, who curtseyed and left the room. Knowing there was little more she could do with the onset of darkness, she turned to Imogene. "We must go down to supper with a brave face. Do not mention our arrangement with Annie to Cousin Esmé. She is determined to believe the worst about our companions."

Imogene clutched Julia's hand, shadows of worry in her green eyes. "What if they are not discovered tonight? I tell you I care not a whiff for this fortune if Roderick has disappeared."

Knowing exactly how the young lady felt, Julia replied, "I for one intend to be on horseback when dawn breaks if they have not returned. No amount of money could compensate for the loss of my dearest friend, and so I shall tell Esmé if she tries to stop me on the morrow."

Margie, who'd quietly stood by the dresser during the meeting of the ladies, interjected, "Lady Powers wouldn't be pleased to 'ear you sayin' that, miss. She's countin' on you to inherit."

"There is little I do that pleases my mother. In this instance, I intend to follow my conscience."

Julia held her head high as she led Imogene out of the room. She hadn't given up on her friend, but caution told her they must wait until morning to look for the missing pair. The intervention of Annie and her brothers had gone far to reconcile her to not searching that night. If Esmé disapproved, then so be it, for she would not be swayed from her path.

Sir Gordon struggled with the golden curl on his forehead. What did Ryland do to make it stand just so? He picked up his silver brush and worked for a moment on the errant tress, then sighed with disgust when the curl sagged back to lay flat. He would be forced to send his regrets unless his man returned soon.

Tossing the brush on the dresser in disgust, he flopped onto the closest chair. Soon a smile settled on his handsome face. Matters couldn't have turned out better. He was certain that Miss Powers and Miss Shelton were going to do something to disgrace themselves with Cousin Esmé.

The door to the baronet's chamber opened, and a breathless Ryland entered. "Sorry to be late, sir."

Sir Gordon started up, clapping his man on the shoulder. "You have done an excellent job, old fellow." Suddenly looking at his hand which came away covered with dirt, he stepped back. "Why, you are as filthy as a grave digger." He stopped, before nervously asking, "They are unharmed, are they not?"

"Didn't have to touch a hair on their heads, sir." Ryland chuckled. He really should have gone on the stage, instead of catering to the whims of a dandy. He'd had the major and the lady in a quake with his disguise and his coarse accent. He really ought to thank the chattering

Trudie for telling him about the old cottage and the cellar. But since she didn't know she'd helped him, there was really no point in wasting his breath. "Hardest part was catchin' them horses and leavin' them in the village. But all has been taken care of."

"Excellent, but you must help me dress, for I don't want to miss anything tonight."

Ryland removed his own dirty jacket as the baronet watched. "That fool Willet gave me a green horse that tossed me in dirt. Likely, he'll be a fine animal when fully trained—and fast. Luckily, the lady and the major were already on foot when I came upon them. They're safely locked in an abandoned cottage on the far side of the estate."

Sir Gordon nodded, then waited as Ryland picked up the brush and began to work his magic. "How did you manage to arrange the carriage and the mysterious pair in the village so quickly? " 'Twas a stroke of genius, I must say. That alone convinced Esmé to suspend the search."

"Couple? I don't know anythin' about a couple but the major and Miss Fields. You shan't see them afore the morrow, I swear."

Sir Gordon gave a shout of laughter. "Why, 'twas but a stroke of good fortune that the pair were leaving just at that moment. Upon my soul, Ryland, I think fate is on my side. I *shall* inherit Cousin Esmé's fortune. See if I don't."

# *Ten*

Roderick tightened his arms around the sleeping woman. The intoxicating scent of wildflowers clung to her. She felt soft and warm as he held her against his chest, filling him with a desire to kiss her awake. He struggled to keep his thoughts from the lusty longings which lay just below the surface as she pressed so innocently against him.

To distract himself, he let his tired gaze sweep the cellar's shadowy corners, then came to rest on the last candle, now half-burned on the bench beside them. They would have to await rescue in darkness, a rather unpleasant prospect.

Wondering if they would be found soon, he gazed at the trapdoor. The sturdy portal had resisted all his efforts to break out. Despite its solid construction, thin points of light once again showed through the cracks. Dawn had broken and hopefully a search for them had begun by now.

Miss Fields stirred in his arms. With a start, she sat upright and looked at him. Her blue eyes were unfathomable in the dim light, but he sensed she was startled to find herself in his arms. As her gaze dropped to her clasped hands, he thought her more beautiful than ever with her rich brown hair tumbling below her shoulders in a mass of disheveled curls.

"You should have awakened me, sir. I did not mean to inconvenience you in such a manner." Elizabeth's emotions were in turmoil. How had she come to be in the major's arms? The feel of those strong arms made her feel safe and comfortable, but a strange desire had surged forth in her to put her arms around the gentleman and press her lips to his. It had been a shocking thought, which caused her to bolt up and away from his disturbing influence.

"I was glad to offer my services, Miss Fields, for I am certain you were quite fatigued after so much excitement and fear." The kind grin only made the major appear more devastatingly handsome.

Too close to the gentleman for her own peace of mind, Elizabeth rose and walked towards the stone stairs. She looked up to see tiny rays of light. "We have been here the entire night?"

"Yes. I am certain they will begin a search now that it's dawn. I hope you had no nightmares from your experiences yesterday."

Elizabeth shook her head. "I don't believe I dreamed at all, I was so exhausted. The last thing I remember was wondering who might be behind our imprisonment. 'Tis clear your ghost and our brigand are working for the same person." She was silent for a moment, then added with a wry smile, "I know you have acquitted me of attempting to frighten your sister, but who do you think played the ghost?"

"I believe a maid named Trudie was convinced to don the sheet. Miss Powers stated the girl was quite enamored with Sir Gordon's man and would very likely have willingly enacted the part."

"Trudie? Sir, I don't think so, unless your ghost was very short and stout." Elizabeth had chanced upon the maid in the hallway and was startled at the girl's girth.

The major frowned and looked into the flickering

flame. "Was there another maid who might have agreed to help Sir Gordon or his valet?"

"I cannot say for certain there is not, for servants are always susceptible to bribes. But Annie, one of Miss Langley's maids, swears that except for Trudie, the staff holds the baronet and his man in strong dislike."

"Then I am at a loss about who came to my sister's room. As for our brigand, either Mrs. Bradford or Sir Gordon could have paid the man."

Elizabeth came back to the small circle of light. "I think we must try to discover who played the ghost. Tell me what happened in Imogene's room that night."

Roderick quickly detailed the story of his encounter with the spirit in his sister's room. He revealed all except his lying in wait for the lady he falsely thought the culprit.

When he'd finished, Elizabeth nodded, then turned to pace the small area several times before she paused. "And you say that the door in the second room was locked?"

"It was and that puzzles me." Roderick liked the way she worried her lower lip with her teeth as she paced. Would those lips taste as sweet as he imagined?

"Major, do you remember what Miss Langley told us about the house the first night of our visit? She said it had some unusual features. Perhaps there is a secret panel in that room."

Roderick's brows rose. "Miss Fields, Langley Hall is barely a century old. There would have been no need for Priest Holes and the like when the structure was designed. Miss Langley said the interior design was by Hawksmoor. I cannot see a man who is famous for his cathedrals and public buildings being involved in such a childish creation as secret panels and passageways."

"True, but Miss Langley's grandmother obviously had a Gothic turn of mind. She might have had secret passageways included for her own amusement. Besides, we know she hired someone to alter Hawksmoor's original design."

"But even if we agree that is possible, how does that help us determine who was our ghost?"

"We must find the panel and see what there is to discover in the passageways. Who knows? It might lead us to the very person who is behind the conspiracy."

" 'Tis very likely that whoever played the ghost won't do so again," Roderick replied doubtfully.

"Anyone who would go to such lengths as to lock us in this cellar is not likely to give up after we are found. Mark my words, we have not seen the last of your ghost."

"Ah, but my dear Miss Fields, that is the crux of the problem. Unless we get out of here, we are not likely to see anyone." The major crossed his arms and leaned back against the stone wall as if there was no help for their situation.

"Then we must do something to help them find us." Elizabeth began to search around on the dirt floor. She could barely see anything, but at last she found what she needed. She picked up a piece of wood from a broken brandy keg; it still reeked of the odor of spirits. "We shall hammer on the door. If anyone comes into the meadow they cannot fail to hear us."

Roderick shook his head, amazed at her continued optimism. "Allow me to do that, Miss Fields."

Elizabeth stepped away from the gentleman. In a firm voice, she declared, "I shall begin. When I am tired you may take my place."

The lady stood still for a few moments, taking in several deep breaths as if gaining some strength of resolve with each gulp of air.

Filled with admiration for her determination and stamina, Roderick knew she must be as hungry and tired as he was, yet she did not complain. As she finished her deep breathing, he inquired, "Do you feel more the thing?"

"Very much so, but I don't think I would recommend dank air for breaking one's fast 'Tis not the least bit filling." Elizabeth's eyes twinkled as she turned and marched up the stairs to the trapdoor.

"True, but only think how slimming it must be. Perhaps we should recommend it to the Prince of Wales."

Elizabeth's laughter rang out in the cellar; the sound warmed Roderick's heart. He knew their lighthearted attempts at humor were to keep their fears at bay. Would they be rescued? As he watched the resourceful Miss Fields begin to rap on the door sharply with the barrel plank, he thought she was just the kind of lady whom one would chose if one must be stranded for the night.

Good heavens! The implications of being with the unchaperoned lady all night suddenly struck him with the force of a French musket ball.


Julia tapped softly on the heavy oak door. "Are you awake, Imogene?"

Within seconds, Miss Shelton threw the door open with harried impatience. The young lady had opted not to ring for a maid for fear one would inform Miss Langley of their plans.

Imogene looked only half-dressed with her red hair loose about her shoulders and the grey jacket to her riding habit still laying on her bed. "I slept later than I meant to, but I shall be ready as soon as I braid my hair."

Hoping to hurry matters along, Julia offered to assist Imogene, and within ten minutes the younger lady was neatly, if somewhat plainly, dressed for their ride. Julia hoped that her trepidation at this defiance of Esmé's orders was not visible in her demeanor as they came down the stairs in the Great Hall.

Spying Aegis bellowing orders at several footmen, the young ladies hurried down to see if there was news. The old man quickly informed them they must direct their questions to his mistress in the breakfast parlour. In truth, he could barely hear one in ten words, for their speech was too soft and rapid.

When the butler moved away, Imogene tugged at the sleeve of Julia's unfashionable green habit. "Must we see our cousin before we leave? Why, she all but abandoned Roderick and Elizabeth to their fates last evening. Besides, she will likely try to stop us."

"True, but I believe we should let her know what we intend. She cannot refuse on the grounds of darkness anymore." So saying, Julia led the nervous, but defiant Imogene to the small parlour at the rear of the house.

The young ladies entered the room to discover Sir Gordon having a *tête-à-tête* with Esmé at the table. He fell silent immediately upon spying them. He arched one golden brow as he took in their attire, and a smirk settled on his handsome features.

"My dear girls, you are up rather early." Esmé frowned when she took note of their riding habits. "Don't tell me you still believe your friend and brother are lost on the estate somewhere?"

"We do, Cousin Esmé." Julia was surprised at the steadiness of her speech, for her knees felt quite shaky. "Imogene and I intend to search for them this morning. We don't believe there has been an elopement."

Sir Gordon snickered. "One never wishes to acknowledge that our friends or relatives are unworthy."

Julia heard Imogene draw breath to issue a stinging retort, but she squeezed the girl's hand which rested on her arm. There was no point in antagonizing anyone. Only the return of Elizabeth and Major Shelton would prove them right.

Esmé picked up her cup. Staring into the brew, she

nonchalantly asked, "You still intend to go, knowing I disapprove?"

"We do, Cousin Esmé. If you knew the lost pair as Imogene and I do, you would not have suspended the search last night. We are sorry to disoblige you, but they need—"

The parlour door opened and Aegis entered the room with a silver tray on which a sealed note rested. "A man brought a message from Major Shelton, I believe."

Imogene and Julia instinctively stepped forward as Miss Langley lifted her lorgnette to read the front of the note. Shaking her head, she laid the missive on the table unopened and shouted, "Not *from* the major, Aegis, *for* him."

The old man shrugged his shoulders and left the room, muttering about people needing to speak plainer.

Imogene's heart was in a flutter as her gaze rested on the letter. Was Roderick being called back to his regiment so soon? With trembling fingers, she picked up the message. Reading the front, her relief was so great she unconsciously spoke aloud. " 'Tis from Kirtland Grange. No doubt, my uncle writes to inform Roderick that his marriage has taken place. I shall see that my brother gets this." She tucked the note into the pocket of her riding habit.

Sir Gordon taunted, "Now, you will have two marriages to celebrate when your brother and his wife return from Scotland. But then, perhaps your uncle will not wish to acknowledge such an . . . indiscreet affair."

Seeing the angry red flags of warning rise on Imogene's cheeks, Julia interceded to prevent the girl from saying things which, while relieving her ire, she might later regret. "We shall not argue about whether there has been an elopement or not, Sir Gordon. Imogene and I intend to ride about the estate and look for ourselves." Turning to her cousin, she added, "I know you disapprove, madam, but we are not endangering ourselves. We are convinced that they remain out there in some kind of trouble."

Esmé's eyes darkened, but there was no rebuke. "Very well, but I shall expect to see you both at nuncheon. Is that understood?"

Convinced they would know something by then, one way or the other, Julia agreed. "I promise we shall return no later than one o'clock."

"Tell Shaw what you wish, carriage or horse, and make certain he accompanies you."

The young ladies thanked their cousin before quickly exiting the room. Sir Gordon sat back and eyed his cousin closely. He noted the slight puckering around her mouth and was certain the two young ladies were now quite out of favor. "Don't be disappointed in your relatives, my dear cousin. The folly of youth is being always certain of being right."

Esmé grasped her cane, using the ebony stick to rise. She was concerned. What if she was wrong about the missing couple? What if they'd lain injured during the night instead of traveling to Scotland? It didn't bear thinking about. She'd summon Willet and have him inquire further about the couple who'd entered the carriage. "Well, I am not certain one ever gets past that failing, Sir Gordon. You will excuse me, for I have business in the library."

After his cousin's departure, the baronet treated himself to a second cup of coffee, basking in his success. Now all he had to do was await the arrival of Miss Myra Bradford to the breakfast parlour. He would use his considerable charms. If he wasn't mistaken, the lady would be his by tonight, a thought which surprisingly sent the blood rushing to his loins.

The fog hung low over the River Nidd as Cyril and Rufus Brock tramped along the banks, their lanterns now extinguished as the sun edged over the tops of the trees. They'd been set on their course when their little sister, Annie, had arrived at the family cottage early last night and had begged their assistance in looking for a soldier and a young lady missing from Langley. When her soft entreaties hadn't persuaded them to forsake their beds, she'd threatened never again to bring them treats from Cook at the Hall nor to cook for them herself.

Cyril, being the oldest, had eyed his favorite apple tartlets in the basket Annie brought, and the decision was quickly made. The two young shepherds had set out almost at once.

The men were exhausted and hungry after the long night of searching. They had gone their separate ways and visited nearly every remote spot they could remember on the Langley estate without success. Now, with the coming of dawn, they came together and knew that they must return to their flocks. But not before going to their cottage for a tankard of ale and a slice of cheese and bread.

Even as they made their way homeward for their meal, Cyril questioned his brother as to where he'd looked. "Did ye think to look in at Green 'Ollow?"

"Aye, 'twas empty as a witch's 'eart."

"And at the glen on Lang's Tor?"

"Not a twig disturbed."

Cyril shook his head. The couple seemed to have vanished. "Well, we done our best, lad. Likely 'tis all a take-in by this 'ere soldier. Let's go back for a bite afore we get to work."

The men turned west from the river and began to work their way through the woods back to their own snug abode. They'd gone barely a mile into the forest when Rufus gave a shout. "Look, Cyril, on the ground!"

Cyril followed the direction his brother indicated and spied a lady's beaver hat with a white scarf tangled among the weeds in the middle of the small clearing. Within minutes they found a gentleman's hat some feet away lying near a small elm tree. Cyril knew they were on the right trail. They quickly began a search of the area and Rufus discovered hoof marks leading due west.

"Where's this 'ere lane lead?" Rufus called to his brother as they hurried along the overgrown path.

"Remember old Cray. Afore he died, he lived in a small cottage out 'ere with his daughter. Some says she was a witch. Place burnt a few years after he passed when 'twas struck by lightnin'. The girl disappeared and no folks want to live where there be strange doin's. Some say the place be evil."

Rufus shuddered. He didn't want to be disturbing any spirits. He'd just hang back and let Cyril handle things, just the way his brother liked.


Roderick gazed into the flame of the nearly spent candle, his mind numb with the shock. The sound of Miss Fields still pounding on the locked door barely penetrated his stunned thoughts.

Honour demanded that he marry the lady! He looked up to see her pause from her hammering to listen intently for outside sounds, but when his gaze slid to the white hollow of her neck, exposed by her partially opened collar, something intense flared within him at the thought of burying his lips on that tender spot.

He forced his eyes back to the safety of the flame. He could ill afford the responsibility of a wife. His small resources were strained providing for Imogene and himself. But he had no choice, he must do the honourable thing.

*Marriage.* The very thing he'd vowed never to do. As thoughts of calling Elizabeth Fields his wife filled his mind, he couldn't muster any outrage or distress. Why? Because from the very first he'd been drawn to this woman, against his will, against his better judgment, and against his assertions to remain unaffected.

None of that mattered now. He must do his duty and—

The lady's hand touched his shoulder startling him out of his thoughts. "Major, is something wrong?"

While he'd been lost in thought, she'd come to stand beside him. Roderick saw the curiosity in the lady's blue eyes. He rose, and placed his hands on her shoulders, looking down at her with compassion. She didn't even seem to realize that a single night had changed her destiny. "Miss Field, I . . ."

Elizabeth, looking at the major with concern, was startled when the candle guttered out. The cellar was plunged into total darkness. A sudden feeling of panic filled her at the thought of endless hours locked in the cellar's murky depths.

With little thought, she stepped into the circle of Major Shelton's arms, pressing her face into his broad chest. Her terror was replaced with a warmth surging through her veins as the soldier's heartbeat sounded in her ear and the smell of sandalwood filled her lungs. She felt safe, but something she'd never known before was stirring deep within her.

His husky voice came to her as his breath brushed the top of her hair. "Miss Fields?"

She drew back to peer up at him. Was he experiencing the same rush of emotions as she? Her eyes, now more accustomed to the darkness, could barely make out the pale outline of his face in the dim light filtering through the trapdoor. But she could see no hint to his thoughts.

Holding her, Roderick's senses were overwhelmed. The feel of Elizabeth in his arms sent the blood roaring in his ears. He knew these sensations were about desire, not duty or honour. He wanted her. But it was more than that, he loved her. He brought his hand up and caressed the nape of her neck, claiming her lips as he crushed her against him.

His kiss deepened when he felt the eagerness of her response. He knew no thoughts or worries about the future and the difficulties they would face. He only savoured the waves of pleasurable sensations.

A sound from above broke the spell and the pair drew apart. Elizabeth was breathless as she stared through the darkness at the man who'd just embraced her. Her thoughts were not of rescue but of her actions. Her cheeks warmed as she remembered her wanton surrender to his kiss. She turned her back to him, unable to face him due to her reckless behavior.

The cellar door was suddenly thrown open, flooding the cell-like room with blinding morning light. A coarse voice called, "Be there anyone down there?"

The major seemed to start from the trance he'd fallen into after the kiss. Shielding his eyes, he went to the stairs. "Thank God, someone has come. We were locked in here by a brigand."

Elizabeth stood at the edge of the shaft of light which now filled the cellar. She placed her hands over her face as if protecting her eyes from its brightness, but in truth, it was a mere ruse to cover her confusion at the realization that she'd fallen in love with the major. She couldn't hold him in affection. What about her responsibility to Sarah and Ruth? Nevertheless, despite her best intentions, and with the least amount of encouragement on his part, she'd fallen hopelessly in love with Major Shelton.

"Miss Fields, are you ready to get out of here at last?"

His voice sounded strained to her. No doubt he was already regretting the impulse to kiss her in the dark. She wasn't even certain he liked her, for too often he'd seemed to disapprove of her. A shudder of humiliation ran through her at what he must have thought of her eager response to his embrace.

Squaring her shoulders, she dropped her hands from her face, determined not to reveal the extent of her emotions. She avoided looking at the gentleman who'd managed to steal her heart. Instead, she moved past him up the stairs and into the glaring morning light.

A rough hand grasped her own as she came up through the opening, and she found herself being assisted by a large lad who smelled strongly of sheep. His cheerful round face reminded her of someone, but at present her thoughts were so distracted she could not think who.

"Are ye uninjured, miss?"

Elizabeth merely shook her head, then thanked the young man before moving past him out through the cottage door and into the open pasture. She should have been delighted at the smell of the sweet fresh air, but she was still too disturbed by the realization of her folly. She'd fallen in love with a man who, according to his sister, had no intention of ever marrying.

Restlessly, she moved about through the tall grass, trying to keep her thoughts from the major. Chills seemed to surge through her, far worse ones than when she'd been down in that damp hole.

As Roderick emerged from the cellar, he could see Elizabeth walking in front of the cottage, her arms folded about her as if she were still cold. She'd barely said a word since he'd kissed her. What were her thoughts? Did she mistakenly think he'd been trying to take advantage of the situation? Or was she concerned that he wouldn't do the honourable thing and marry her? He needed to get her alone so they could resolve this misunderstanding.

Aware of the large lad waiting expectantly beside him, Roderick turned and distractedly inquired, "Who do we have to thank for our release?"

"Cyril Brock, sir. I work for Miss Langley, but me sister,

Annie, sent us to look for ye and the lady. Me brother's out there in the meadow. Lad took a notion that this place was 'aunted and wouldn't come in."

"No matter, Cyril. We are grateful for your assistance. Did you bring a horse or carriage? I don't think Miss Fields will be able to walk all the way back to the Hall."

The young shepherd pulled his hat from his head, leaving his thin brown hair pointed in several directions. "Didn't think to bring one, sir, but Rufus and I'll run back to the 'all and we'll 'ave ye out of 'ere in a trice."

Before Roderick could agree, the young man hurried from the burned-out building and crossed the pasture to where his brother waited. The pair quickly disappeared down a pair of carriage ruts which led into the forest.

Coming to the door, the major watched Elizabeth as she walked among the wildflowers in the meadow. Her thick brown hair sparkled with golden glints in the morning sun as she stooped to pluck a daisy. She reminded him of an elusive wood nymph that might escape him if he weren't careful.

Pushing such fanciful thoughts from his mind, he strode to where she stood with her back to him. "Miss Fields, we must speak before the others return."

The lady looked at him with shuttered blue eyes. Her tone was polite, but decidedly cool. "Major Shelton, I must thank you for your protection during this harrowing event."

Her manner was not encouraging, but Roderick persisted. "Miss Fields . . . Elizabeth, I must tell you that your kiss—"

"Sir, don't be so unkind as to remind me." The lady gave a brittle laugh as she looked away from him. "I was very frightened when the candle went out, and you must attribute my actions to that. I hold you under no obligation—"

Roderick, losing patience with her cool demeanor,

grasped her by the shoulders, turning her to face him. He wanted to kiss her again until she was breathless, but her face was a mask of icy composure. He suspected he was making a mess of this proposal, but his anger now ruled his actions. "The circumstances, my dear, are not to be ignored. You can be certain that no one else will disregard the fact that we have been out here in each other's company all night. Elizabeth, you *must* marry me!"

# *Eleven*

Elizabeth's misery on hearing those words was so acute, it was nearly a physical ache. He didn't love her. He only wanted to protect her honour. Having witnessed the joy of her parents' love match, the mere idea of marrying a man under lesser circumstances was unthinkable.

Gathering her wits, she tried to pull from his grasp, but his fingers only tightened, preventing her escape. "Don't be ridiculous, Major. We shan't see each other again once we leave Langley Hall. You will return to your unit and I to my family. Save the few people staying with Miss Langley, no one need know about this misadventure. There is no necessity for such a sacrifice on your part."

"Sacrifice! Elizabeth, I realize I have done this very badly. My proposal is not about—" Roderick halted abruptly as a shout sounded behind him.

His hands dropped as he turned to see Miss Powers tooling a curricle up the overgrown lane. Hanging behind her on the backstrap were Cyril Brock and his brother. Imogene and a groom followed the carriage on horseback.

Filled with a sense of urgency, Roderick tenderly grasped Elizabeth's hand. "Dear lady, I know you are overwrought after your experience, but please forgive my abruptness. Say you will marry me. You must realize that you have stolen—"

"I cannot, sir." Not allowing him to continue, Elizabeth tugged her hand free and hurried past him towards the approaching party.

Roderick followed behind, cursing the fact that their rescuers hadn't given him a quarter of an hour more. He was certain he could have convinced Elizabeth they should be married.

Julia reined the carriage to a halt. "Mr. Brock, pray hold the horses."

Annie's two burly brothers climbed down from the carriage. Cyril lumbered forward to hold the team. While Julia waited, she eyed her friend with concern. Elizabeth looked tired and disheveled, her hat was missing, and her lovely blue riding habit was covered with dirt and cobwebs. But what concerned Julia the most was the look of total despair on her friend's face. What had happened to leave her in such a state?

Imogene and Shaw drew their horses up beside the carriage. The young girl slid from her mount and rushed to throw herself into her brother's arms. "Roderick, we were so worried. It was such a relief when we came upon Annie's brothers and they told us they had found you."

Julia jumped down from the carriage, going to her friend. Giving her a hug, she then held Elizabeth at arm's length. "Annie's brother said you were locked in the cellar of that cottage. Who would do such a thing?"

Elizabeth could only shake her head as she shrugged her shoulders. Words were beyond her at this point. She wanted to get back to the solitude of her room at the Hall before Major Shelton again voiced his obligation to marry her. She could feel his gaze on her even as Imogene questioned him about what had happened.

As the major gave a quick account of the chain of events that had ended with their incarceration, Julia's expression filled with concern for what the unfortunate pair had experienced. Elizabeth knew her friend needed some reassurance of her well-being, but she was too over-whelmed with despair at the moment. "I am too tired to think properly. Can we not return to the Hall?"

Suddenly the major was at her side, his voice gentle but demanding. "Miss Fields, I must speak to you . . . after you have rested."

Elizabeth couldn't bring herself to look into his com-pelling green eyes. She wouldn't allow herself to weaken her resolve with thoughts of what might be if only he loved her. "I have made my decision, sir, There is no more to be said on the subject."

Suddenly Elizabeth burst into tears. Roderick longed to take her in his arms, but her friend was before him. Julia Powers gazed at him over the distraught woman's head, a look of sympathy on her face.

"Don't worry, Major, Lizzie needs rest and food; then she will come about. I shall take her in the carriage. I'll send someone back for you. We shall worry about other matters later." Julia led her weeping friend towards the curricle.

Shaw, who'd stood quietly holding the mounts during the reunion, stepped forward, handing the reins to the soldier. "No need, miss. Major Shelton can take me 'orse. 'Tis only right, for I shouldn't 'ave let Miss Fields out o' me sight yesterday."

Roderick shook his head as he watched Elizabeth settle on the leather seat of the vehicle. "Don't blame yourself, man. You would have ended up in that cellar the same as us. Go along with Miss Powers."

Taking up the reins from the splash board as Shaw climbed up behind, Julia thanked Annie's brothers, ask-ing them to pay her a visit at the manor that afternoon for their reward. She ordered the sheepherder to stand clear, then with a last encouraging glance at Roderick, she deftly turned the carriage around and drove back up the overgrown lane.

The major thanked the Brock brothers and watched them disappear into the forest. As he stood, lost in thought, Imogene came to stand beside him, a look of curiosity on her elfin face.

"What was Elizabeth talking about?"

Roderick, tired and much out of temper, snapped, "The significance of spending a night alone with Miss Fields cannot escape even an innocent like yourself."

Frowning, Imogene glanced in the direction in which the carriage had disappeared. Her face cleared, and she gave a pleased giggle. "Why, you shall have to make Elizabeth my sister-in-law." She smiled delightedly up at the prospect, but seeing her brother's dark look, she rounded on him with a determined glint in her green eyes. "You cannot mean to refuse to offer for her, no matter your thoughts on a soldier having a wife."

"You very much mistake the matter, Genie. I did offer, but the lady has refused me. Now, let me put you on your saddle before I fall asleep where I stand."

"Refused you! How can that be? I am convinced that she likes you above all others, for there is a certain look that comes into her eyes when she gazes at you. She should have been delighted." Imogene fell into thought as her brother led her to her horse, then gave her a lift up. A sudden frown on her face, she glared down at him. "Unless you took liberties with her in that cellar?"

Roderick glanced guiltily away from his sister. In truth he couldn't completely deny her accusations. He had taken advantage of Elizabeth when he'd kissed her, but he couldn't bring himself to regret it. Seeing Imogene's accusing gaze, he simply chose to ignore her question. "I am tired and don't wish to discuss the matter."

A look of delight settled on Imogene's face. "You kissed her!"

"You pry into matters that are none of your concern."

"I am right! I know I am! Why, Roderick David Shelton,

you are forever going on to me about the proprieties, and now I find you are a rake in disguise."

Roderick mounted his horse, then urged the animal forward. He gave his sister a dark look, and his tone implied a warning. "Genie."

Imogene's eyes twinkled. "You are a rake. I shall have to write Martha Worthingham, for she was forever bragging what a dashing swell her brother was—"

"You will do no such thing, young lady. Remember you would be slandering your future sister-in-law's name even more than mine."

A stricken look crossed the young lady's face. "I would not wish to do anything that would harm Elizabeth, for I am delighted she shall be part of our family. That is, if you can convince her to have you."

"You are not being helpful with this useless chatter, and I am too tired to think what to do just now."

Imogene fell into thought for a few moments as she guided her horse to come abreast of her brother; then she looked earnestly at Roderick. "I know who can help. Julia will know how to bring Elizabeth around. They are the best of friends."

"Perhaps you are correct." There had been something in Miss Powers's final glance that suggested she would aid him. Hope filled Roderick. He could make Elizabeth his.

"Of course, I am. Take my word for it. Women understand these things, dear brother . . . rake." Imogene gave a giggle, then kicked her horse into a canter.

"I am not a rake," Roderick shouted, but his sister only gave a wave of her hand as she galloped away from him. Was that what Elizabeth thought of him? If that were the case, he must change her mind. With a renewed sense of determination, he urged his horse towards the Hall. He would get the lady to agree to marry him. He loved her and wouldn't give up until he possessed her, body and soul.

\* \* \*

"This is dreadful," Esmé said, as the footman left the Egyptian Drawing Room, where she'd come to await word on Julia and Imogene's search. The servant had informed her that Miss Fields and Major Shelton, having been discovered early that morning locked in the cellar of the Cray cottage, were now both returned to the Hall. "I should have continued the search when the young ladies declared an elopement impossible," she added.

Sir Gordon, who'd been like a shadow all day, came to pat her shoulder. "Don't blame yourself. We were all fooled into believing there had been an elopement. There was no harm done, and they are back safe, if somewhat tired."

Miss Hartman angrily puffed out her cheeks. "No harm, sir? Why, Miss Fields's reputation is ruined."

"But, my dear lady, that can easily be remedied if the major is willing to do the honourable thing." The baronet flashed a smile that didn't reach his eyes, before adding, "But then, we cannot be certain he will, not knowing his character."

Esmé shook her head in dismay. "I almost wish it had been an elopement."

"Esmé, you cannot mean that!" Prudence, who'd been staring out the window to avoid looking at all the heathen Egyptian artifacts, rounded on her employer, a look of outrage on her thin face.

"Oh, but I do. With an elopement, we would have been certain they were in love. Now, we know only that they must marry for propriety. 'Tis too sad." The lady sighed.

"Such romantically foolish notions you have, Esmé. I am certain . . ." Prudence halted as the major entered the room. The gentleman looked tired, but he'd taken the time to shave and change into a simple black coat with a grey- and black-striped waistcoat.

"Miss Langley, you requested to see me."

"I did, Major. Pray, tell me what happened to you and Miss Fields yesterday."

Roderick eyed the trio before him. Miss Langley appeared interested, but concerned. Miss Hartman's face was full of suspicion, while Sir Gordon looked as if he'd been dealt a winning hand in cards. Ignoring the two who stood on either side of the heiress like mismatched bookends, the major quickly told Miss Langley the story.

Esmé sat forward as he finished. "You were unable to identify this man?"

"He was fully disguised, and he spoke with the accents of a ruffian. But I am certain he was hired by someone here at the Hall, for he said, as much."

Sir Gordon straightened, a frown marring his handsome features. "Major, I hope you are not accusing my cousin."

"No, Miss Fields and I thought perhaps you or Mrs. Bradford more likely to be the employer."

"Major Shelton, I demand an . . ." The baronet began to bluster, but Esmé placed a restraining hand on his arm.

"We shall have none of that pistols at twenty paces business, Sir Gordon. In truth, you and Myra's mother are the persons most likely to benefit from such a wicked trick."

"Cousin, I am wounded you would think such a thing." Sir Gordon turned away from the lady as if her words had cut out his heart.

"No, you are not," Esmé countered, "but you would be if I allowed you to force the major into a duel."

The baronet blanched at the thought. He had no wish to duel anyone, but he felt he must make some show to appear innocent. "If it is your wish, then I shall refrain from requesting an apology, Cousin, no matter how sorely I am impugned."

"Very good. Now both of you leave me with the major."

After Miss Hartman and Sir Gordon were gone, Esmé encouraged the soldier to be seated. She leaned forward, an edge to her voice as she queried, "What are your plans with regard to Miss Fields, Major?"

"I know my duty. I consider myself engaged to the lady, but at present she is unwilling to agree."

"Duty! Is that how you asked her? No wonder the lady is reluctant to marry if you used such a daunting word. Have you no tender emotions for her, young man?"

Roderick glanced out the window, a vision of Elizabeth's face in his mind's eye. "Yes, I . . . love her."

Esmé relaxed back into her chair, the heaviness now lifted from her. "But you have gone and made a muddle of things with your talk of duty, and she has refused. Very likely she would not even believe you, were you to tell her of your true feeling now. Well, dear boy, how shall you handle this, for I tell you I want this settled. I won't be responsible for sending that girl back to her father with her reputation shattered."

"I have a plan, but I must speak to Miss Powers, for I shall need her assistance."

Esmé gestured for him to be off. "I shall expect good news by this evening, Major. Is that understood?"

Roderick fully took her meaning. Very likely Miss Powers or his sister's chance to inherit rested on a betrothal announcement. But his thoughts were of Elizabeth. Did she love him? Would she at last agree to be his wife? He only knew he had to change her mind.

Excusing himself, he went to the library, where he quickly penned a note requesting Miss Powers meet him while Elizabeth slept. He hoped that lady would assist him. If she truly cared about Elizabeth she would. After he gave the message to a footman, he slumped into the chair behind the large oak desk to await the lady's arrival. He was tired and he must sleep, but he wouldn't retire

until Miss Powers agreed to arrange to have Elizabeth
meet him before dinner.

Elizabeth's hand hesitated over the door handle. How
had she allowed Julia to convince her she must meet with
Major Shelton before the others came down? Had she
taken leave of her senses? She almost drew her hand away
and left; then Julia's words echoed in her mind. "Do it
for my sake. Cousin Esmé is quite adamant that you and
the major must do the right thing. She even hinted that
your decision might affect the outcome of her choosing
either myself or Imogene."

Somehow it all seemed so unfair. She had come to help
Julia, and all she had done so far was to harm her friend's
chances. Taking a deep breath, she grasped the brass handle and entered the library.

Her heart turned in her chest as she saw the major
standing by an open casement window, dressed for dinner
in his red military tunic. As he turned to look expectantly
at her, she was surprised to see his easy smile. What was
there to smile about in this disastrous situation?

"Good evening, Elizabeth." Roderick thought her
beautiful in the cream silk gown trimmed with green ribbons, rosebuds nestled in her brown curls. "Would you
care for something to drink while we talk?"

The lady merely shook her head. "What did you wish
to speak of, sir?"

"Shall we be seated?" Seeing the way her gaze nervously darted about the room, avoiding his, Roderick decided he must approach the matter with caution. Once
he was ensconced opposite Elizabeth, he asked her several commonplace questions. When she began to answer,
she appeared less anxious as she reassured him about her
state of recovery from their ordeal. At last, feeling the
time was right, he got to the point. "Do you think it wise

to disturb Miss Langley's peace of mind this way? She feels responsible for what has happened."

Elizabeth shook her head. "There is no point in assigning blame. What happened, happened and cannot be changed. I think we should forget about the event and go our separate ways. Miss Langley should not give the matter undue reflection."

"But it weighs heavily upon her. I thought perhaps, at least as long as we are her guests, we might have a temporary betrothal. There is likely to be less local scandal, and it will keep Miss Langley from being upset." Seeing the refusal in her eyes, Roderick added, "Besides, do you not plan to help me search for the secret passageway tonight? There would be no impropriety with my 'betrothed' accompanying me into the strange places in which we might find ourselves."

Elizabeth's instinct was to refuse to engage in subterfuge, but the thought of hunting down the ghost stirred her blood. A mock betrothal? She was certain her father wouldn't approve, but Miss Langley's feelings must be taken into account as well. Elizabeth knew this affair had done neither Imogene's nor Julia's cause any good. They were both still in need of the inheritance, and their cousin had yet shown no preference for any of the young ladies.

Somehow the thought that all these tricks had benefited either Sir Gordon or Miss Bradford ruffled Elizabeth's feathers even more. She would only be playing into their hands by adding to the scandal with a refusal now. She must agree to become betrothed for Julia's sake.

Looking up into the major's handsome face, Elizabeth knew a twinge of disappoint that the engagement wouldn't be real. But, she reminded herself, even if she weren't concerned with her sisters' well-being, the fact remained that the major didn't love her. With an effort she finally said, "Very well, sir. For the sake of everyone involved, we shall say we are betrothed. That will surely assuage Miss Langley's guilt."

A look flashed in the gentleman's green eyes which Elizabeth would have sworn was triumph, but it was gone so fast she convinced herself she'd only imagined it. After all, this would only be a temporary arrangement.

"I think that is the wisest course of action, my dear. Now, shall we cry friends and decide when to begin our adventure?"

Somehow, making plans for their search for the passageway put an end to all of Elizabeth's uneasiness in the major's company. She didn't let her mind dwell on her feelings, only on unmasking their tormentor. They discussed when they would meet and who was the most likely person to be behind all the chicanery of ghosts and highwaymen. For his part the major put the blame on Sir Gordon, while Elizabeth thought Miss Bradford the more likely to benefit since she was the other candidate for the legacy and not the baronet.

Coming to no final conclusion, they joined the others in the Yellow Saloon when the case clock in the hall chimed seven. Roderick announced their betrothal to a chorus of congratulations. Esmé was clearly pleased and ordered champagne to celebrate. There seemed to be a surprisingly festive atmosphere as toasts were made. They were all delighted at the betrothal, but then none knew it was only a farce.

The party's idle conversations were halted by the entry of the head groom over Aegis's loud protests. "Can't go in there, man, they're about to go dine."

"Miss Langley, I got news for ye. About the couple and the fancy rig from Ripley."

Esmé waved the butler away. "What did you discover, Willet?"

" 'Appens it was Mr. Tyler and the Widow Stanley. Goin' to Ripley to get buckled by special license."

"The vicar got married?" Miss Hartman stood still, her face blank with shock.

"Are you certain, Willet?" Esmé asked doubtfully. Mr. Tyler had appeared a settled bachelor, and Mrs. Stanley was practically a stranger in the neighborhood.

The old man nodded. "Aye, ma'am, and that ain't all. Seems the 'appy couple be packin' up right this instant. They intend on goin' to America. The reverend is givin' up the livin' and goin' to be a farmer. Turns out 'is lady used to be a Cit's wife and she's loaded with blunt."

Roderick was suddenly reminded of his conversation with Mr. Tyler about chosen professions. The gentleman hadn't been a very good vicar with his continuous moralizing, perhaps he'd be happier doing something else in America. "I think he will make an excellent farmer with his love of the land."

Esmé nodded, then frowned. "I am certain he will, but now I must find someone to take over the living."

Julia startled everyone by boldly saying, "Elizabeth's father has a young man working under him who has been looking for a parish, Cousin. His name is Mr. Ritter."

"Yes, Miss Langley," Elizabeth added, wishing she'd thought of Julia's beloved first, but her thoughts were somewhat distracted tonight. "My father has only the highest praise for the young man."

"Then I shall write him in the morning. Now, Willet, thank you for coming with that information. I shall speak with you in the morning."

While the old man left, Elizabeth shot a jubilant look at her friend. They had managed to secure a position for a very worthy young man, and should Julia be chosen by Esmé, he would be nearby. If not, Mr. Ritter would now be in a position to offer for the lady of his choice.

The evening soon fell into the usual pattern after dinner. The young ladies took their turn at the pianoforte. Then Sir Gordon read sonnets to the group, all the while putting Miss Bradford to the blush with his bold looks, a fact her mother missed as she pored over a box of sweet-meats the baronet had provided. There was little discussion of the news about Mr. Tyler, for in truth none knew him well.

At last one by one they retired. The evening seemed endless for Elizabeth, for she was eager to begin the search, besides having no wish to discuss her "pending" marriage.

When Julia offered her final congratulations before she left for her chamber, Elizabeth was flooded with guilt for deceiving her friend. Still, it was partly for Julia's own good, and for that she would be thanked later.

"Sir Gordon, you must reconsider. I don't think this is such a wise plan," the valet pleaded as his young master stood admiring himself before the mirror.

"Nonsense, Ryland. I have given the matter a great deal of thought, and I believe this is just the thing to secure the legacy." After satisfying himself he was in looks, the baronet turned and went to the door. "Are you with me?"

The servant shook his head in dismay. He'd spent the last half-hour trying to dissuade Sir Gordon from this foolish path. If the baronet was wrong, they'd lose all they'd worked for. On the other hand, if he was right, Ryland knew he'd finally get his reward for having stayed all these years. With a sigh, he decided he'd best stick with what he knew. "Aye, sir. I'm right behind you."

After what had seemed the longest evening of her life, Elizabeth was at last back in her own room in the west wing. Having slept much of the day, she wasn't the least bit fatigued. She anxiously waited until she heard the clock strike eleven. Only then did she steal into the hall where the sounds of Mrs. Bradford's snoring disturbed the quiet. Making her way to the Main wing where all the prospective candidates for the legacy were lodged, she looked for the signal the major promised to indicate Imogene's room.

Spying a black ribbon tied on a door handle, Elizabeth knew she'd found what she looked for. She scratched softly on the door. The portal opened at once, as if the major had been waiting impatiently on the other side.

He gestured her in, then looked up and down the hall before removing the ribbon and closing the door. "Did you see anyone about?"

Elizabeth shook her head. "All is quiet."

Roderick liked the way her eyes sparkled with excitement in the candlelight when she looked at him. This was the Elizabeth who'd stolen his heart. It made him want to kiss her again, but his cooler self prevailed. He had much to do before he could claim another such token. His own sister had accused him of being a rake, so he must go slowly. "Good. Shall we go next door and begin the search?"

He picked up his candle from the small table by the door and led Elizabeth through the dressing room and into the adjoining chamber. Their candles barely lessened the darkness of the large room.

"What do we look for?" Elizabeth asked, holding her candle high to see better.

"Come, let us begin at the door. You go to the left and I shall look to the right. Merely press on the wood panels, see if something looks out of the ordinary." They went to stand side by side, surveying the wainscoted wall.

On impulse, Roderick tried the door handle. Discovering it was unlocked, he turned the key. Seeing her questioning look, he smiled. "Just making certain we won't be disturbed in our task. I would hate to have to explain to

Miss Hartman that we are engaged in an innocent occupation."

Elizabeth laughed as she stepped to the left and started to run a hand over the oak surface. Roderick watched as she eagerly pushed and prodded the polished panels. He was amazed at her good humor and enthusiasm considering what had happened to them yesterday.

With equal verve, he began to inspect the wall to the right of the door. He worked his way along it. After some fifteen minutes, he began to doubt they would find the passageway or if it even existed.

Coming to a large tapestry depicting a scene from the Crusades, he paused to look back at Elizabeth. She'd set her candle upon a table and was using both hands to test the panels around the marble fireplace. As she raised her arms above her head, her dress molded to the outline of her trim figure, sending a wave of longing through Roderick. Thinking to distract himself, he dropped his gaze to her candle, then offered, "Would you like me to move the table for you?"

Elizabeth stopped what she was doing and turned to him. "Please."

Roderick came forward, handing her his candle and the one from the table. He carefully lifted one end of the heavy oak piece of furniture, moving it out from the wall so she could go behind it.

As he walked round to move the other side, she hesitantly asked, "Do you think we are wasting our time?"

"I feel certain our ghost shall be on the prowl again. No one has been frightened away, and both Imogene and Miss Powers are still very much in contention for the legacy. Time is running out, so something must be done. I want to be there when the ghost shows itself." Roderick finished pulling the table out and came to retrieve his candle. He ignored the tingling of his fingers when they brushed Elizabeth's as the brass candlestick changed hands.

"Do you think the spirit will come to Imogene's chamber again?" Elizabeth stepped back a bit as the major's proximity set her heart to hammering. Why did she have this foolish wish to have him press his lips to hers again?

The major looked around the room that lay in near darkness. "I think whoever is playing the ghost will look for a new victim, but I should like to be in those passageways when he begins his prank."

"He! I know you are convinced that Sir Gordon is the culprit, but you thought the ghost was a woman."

"I don't know who was under the sheet, but I am certain the baronet will be close by if the prank is reenacted."

Elizabeth noted the way Major Shelton's green eyes glittered with menace when he spoke of Sir Gordon. "Do I need to fear for that gentleman's safety if we should discover him in the passageways?"

Roderick looked down at the worried expression on Elizabeth's lovely face. Remembering all that had occurred to both his sister and the lady before him, a surge of anger raced through him. He wanted nothing more than to draw Mondell's cork, but he wouldn't subject Elizabeth to such violence. In a soft but firm tone, he said, "I promise I shall only capture him and take him before his cousin for punishment." If the man got a few extra scrapes and bruises along the way, all the better.

The major had no way of knowing that his gentle reassurances sounded only seductively alluring to Elizabeth. Her gaze dropped to his full firm lips, and she was flooded with the memory of their having taken possession of her own. Angry with her continued fascination with a man who didn't love her, she quickly turned to put a trembling hand on the wall panel. "Then we must find the secret door, for I should like the person responsible to be brought to justice."

Roderick sensed he'd disturbed Elizabeth in some way, but he knew she was right. If the pretender was going to do something it would be soon, so they must get into the hidden passageway. He quickly returned to the embroidered wall hanging where he'd ended his search. Lifting the heavy fabric, he felt the wall, but nothing appeared to be an entry way.

Working his way along the tapestry, he'd reached the halfway point where Richard the Lionhearted led his men to battle against the Moors when a panel gave way under the pressure of his hand. Excitement surged through him, and he straightened to announce his discovery.

Suddenly he checked the impulse. There might be a scuffle if he came upon anyone, and Elizabeth might get hurt. He must go alone. He knew she would be furious when she discovered him missing, but it would be for the best.

Looking about the room, he pondered a way to distract her. Then it came to him. "Are you having any luck?"

She stood up from where she'd been inspecting a panel near the floor. "Not yet."

"Perhaps what we need is more light." The major walked to a brace of unlit candles on a table, then turned, saying, "There is another candelabra like this in Imogene's old room. Would you mind lighting it and bringing it here?"

Elizabeth nodded. "I shall hurry." She picked up her candle from the table, and made her way through the dressing room into the second chamber. It took some minutes to locate the candelabra, which had been set on the far side of the wardrobe.

Taking time to light the five tapers, she lifted the heavy silver brace, and made her way back. Entering the room, she was surprised to see the major's candles still unlit. What had distracted him?

"Major, is something wrong?" Elizabeth called.

There was no answer. She was now quite alone in the room. Major Shelton had disappeared.

# Twelve

Elizabeth's irritation was great at discovering herself alone. Determined not to be left behind, she pulled a straight-backed chair over to the last place the major had been searching. She positioned the large candelabra for best illumination, then began testing the panels covered by the tapestry.

Within minutes, she discovered the hidden passageway behind a panel which pushed inward. She quickly retrieved her single candle and entered the hidden corridor. The waist-level opening forced her to stoop low. Straightening once inside, she inspected the dusty passage. Ancient timbers hung with cobwebs. The air was stale and musty. She was suddenly reminded of the cellar, but she pushed the memories of her night with the major from her mind.

As she stepped forward, her candle illuminated a set of very steep stairs which arched in a semicircle. This passageway used one of the turrets, she realized as she proceeded to climb. When she reached the landing, she followed the narrow corridor, hoping to come upon Major Shelton. She had a thing or two to say to that gentleman about his leaving her behind.

The passageway took several twists and turns before being intersected by a second one. Uncertain which way the major had gone, she lowered the candle to the floor and discovered the dust had been disturbed in the left passageway.

Elizabeth followed the footprints and had gone only a short distance when she noted a dim light ahead. She hurried forward and discovered the major at the bottom of a second set of stairs, but unlike the first set, these dropped straight down, like a ladder. The gentleman appeared to be searching for a way to open the panel into the room beyond, for he pushed and prodded the wall.

Her ire at being abandoned caused her to wrathfully demand, "How could you leave without me, sir?"

Startled, Roderick glanced up to see Elizabeth, looking like an avenging angel as she glared down at him. Despite her angry tone, he didn't regret his decision. "I only meant to protect you." He forced his gaze from her enchanting face, before he forgot all about this cursed ghost business and climbed back up those stairs to take her in his arms. "Blast, I cannot manage to open this door."

"Try the lever above your head." Her tone was less hostile as she studied him with a speculative look.

"You shouldn't be here. It might be dangerous, and I don't want—" His reprimand was cut short by screams emanating from behind the panel. "Go back to Imogene's room where you will be safe," he ordered. He reached up and thrust the lever in the opposite direction. The panel swung inward. He grasped the door and pushed it open, then crouched to step through into the chamber beyond. A sharp tug in his still healing wound reminded him to take care.

The bedchamber he'd entered looked exactly like the one they'd just left, only with pale pink hangings. The screams had ceased, and the major saw Julia Powers huddled against the headboard of her bed, holding a candle as if to ward off an intruder. Following her frightened gaze, he spied the sheet-covered impostor on the opposite side of the room near the door, arms extended forward as if reaching for the young lady in the fourposter.

"Show yourself, coward!" Roderick took a menacing step forward.

The spirit seemed to freeze in place for a second, then suddenly it whirled. The ends of the flowing material fluttered in the breeze as the miscreant yanked open the chamber door. The unknown person disappeared into the outside hallway, slamming the portal shut as it went.

In pursuit at once, Roderick dashed across the large chamber and threw open the portal. He eyed the closed doors along the corridor. An overwhelming sense of frustration filled him, for there was nothing to be seen in either direction. There hadn't been time enough for the masquerading ghost to disappear into one of the rooms.

Logic told him there was another secret entryway near Miss Powers's door. That was the only explanation for the culprit's vanishing so quickly. Langley Hall was likely rife with hidden passageways. The major crossed the corridor and once again set about searching for an entrance.

Elizabeth entered Julia's room just as the major exited. Certain he was in pursuit of the person who was tormenting them, she was tempted to follow him until she noted Julia's ashen face. She went immediately to her friend. "Are you unharmed?"

Julia nodded her head. "I-I feel so foolish. I knew it was Imogene's ghost, but somehow coming out of the darkness the way it did, it terrified me."

Elizabeth understood about darkness making one do strange things. Hadn't she behaved shamefully in that darkened cellar with the major? Dismissing the recurring memory from her mind, she looked at the closed chamber door, eager to follow the Major Shelton now that she was certain Julia was safe.

"We are close to capturing whoever is playing the prank. Do you wish to come?"

Hesitating for only a moment, Julia tossed back the covers and grabbed her wrapper.

Opening the portal, they discovered Major Shelton still inspecting the wall panels of the hallway.

Roderick looked up from the carved woodwork he was examining to see Elizabeth and Miss Powers watching him. "Are you well, Miss Powers?"

Julia nodded and made a weak attempt to smile.

Roderick's thoughts were all on finding the person responsible for these tricks. "I am certain there is another secret doorway here since the ghost disappeared within seconds of entering the hall."

Elizabeth eagerly said, "We shall help you look, Major."

Roderick gestured the women forward as he attempted to twist a cluster of carved grape leaves in the woodwork with no result. The trio worked feverishly searching for a trick lever knowing the culprit was getting away with every minute's delay.

Within a matter of moments, Elizabeth called, "Here it is!" She'd discovered a piece of molding under a Langley family portrait that, when pushed upward, opened a section of wall some feet away.

Roderick stepped to the opening, then stopped to look back at the ladies. He could see excitement in Elizabeth's eyes, but Miss Powers's held a hint of trepidation. He did not want to be responsible for leading either one of them into jeopardy. "Don't follow me. It is too dangerous."

Having said that, he stepped into the open passageway, then pushed the panel closed behind him. He hoped Elizabeth would obey his orders this time. Possibly she would be ruled by the less impetuous Miss Powers who seemed to exert some small influence on the fearless vicar's daughter.

Holding his candle high for better visibility, he hurried down the narrow corridor. As in the first one, there were several twists and turns, but thankfully no intersecting

passages. At last he came to a dead end where he found
a door which led into another room. He reached up and
pushed the lever to release the latch, and the panel swung
inward.

Roderick crouched low and stepped into a bedchamber, then checked at the sight. There, sitting up in bed
with a book, was Miss Hartman, a branch of candles illuminating her with a nearly angelic glow. She wore a white
night dress and had an excessively frilly cap tied over her
frizzy grey hair.

Upon spying the major, the lady dropped the book and
yanked the covers up to her chin. With a look of genuine
horror on her face she shrieked, "Be gone, you evil seducer!"


Elizabeth watched Roderick close the secret panel with
mixed emotions. On the one hand she was delighted that
he cared enough to be concerned for her safety. She'd
known a rush of pleasure when he'd admitted, in the
passageway, why he'd left her behind. He'd wanted to
protect her. It hadn't been merely what he'd said, but
the way he'd gazed up at her. It had been as if he'd caressed her with a look.

But Elizabeth wouldn't be distracted by her foolish
imaginings. She wanted to experience the satisfaction of
capturing their tormentor. She was certain there was little
danger to either Julia or herself. But would her friend
agree to go? "Do we stay here like a pair of frightened
sparrows, or do we help the major?"

Julia nervously clutched her wrapper as Elizabeth
placed a hand on the triggering device for the secret
doorway. "There is nothing wrong with being a frightened sparrow, Lizzie. No doubt they live to be very old
birds."

"Then I shall go by myself." Elizabeth activated the panel and stepped through the opening.

"Oh, I knew you would say that." Remembering all her friend had been through for her sake, Julia rallied her courage. "I cannot let you go alone."

The ladies hurried along the dusty, narrow corridor. Suddenly, Elizabeth stopped as muffled noises penetrated the thick walls. "Do you hear that?"

Julia cocked her head slightly. "Why, I do believe it is Miss Hartman."

Filled with a sense of urgency by the frantic tone of the cries, Elizabeth rushed down the passageway. They came to the end, and she stood on tiptoe to reach the lever that opened the secret panel. By now the shouted words of the lady in the chamber beyond were clear.

"Seducer! Debaucher! Help, someone, or I shall be ravished!"

Pulling the small door open, Elizabeth could hear the major's scornful voice. "Madam, cease your foolish hysterics. I am but looking for someone masquerading as a ghost. A secret passage led me to your chamber."

Elizabeth straightened as she entered Miss Hartman's chamber, stepping forward so Julia could come in behind her. They'd entered on the dark side of the room and neither of the verbal combatants seemed aware of their arrival.

Miss Hartman was in bed, pointing an accusing finger at the major. "Don't think you can enjoy my favors now that you have had your way with Miss Fields, sirrah!"

"Madam, you are the most absurd creature it has ever been my misfortune to meet." Roderick took a menacing step forward. "And allow me to issue you a warning. Don't ever let me hear you defame Miss Fields's name again."

Elizabeth's heart beat faster at the major's tone. Why, he'd defended her so vehemently, one would almost believe he had feelings for her. Was she merely engaging in wishful thinking, or did he truly care for her in some small way? Realizing now was not the time for her personal dilemma, she tried to set her sudden sense of hope aside, but it proved difficult.

A frustrated expression settled on Miss Hartman's thin face at the major's warning. She pulled a handkerchief from her sleeve and sniffled. "You are a monstrous brute, sir!"

Seeing the major's clenched jaw, Elizabeth attempted to calm Miss Hartman. "My dear lady, the major is telling you the truth. We have been searching for a ghost who entered Julia's room, trying to frighten her away from here."

Miss Langley's companion started when she saw Elizabeth and Julia step into the glow of light. Her gaze dropped to her hands, which folded and unfolded her lace handkerchief, and she whined, "Everyone knows the Hall is not haunted. Why, Esmé's father died in London and her mother at their Brighton estate. Ghosts at Langley, what a Banbury story!"

Julia went to stand beside the bed, placing a reassuring hand over the lady's to finally convince the frightened spinster that no one was after her virtue. "Miss Hartman, you misunderstand. We are not saying there was a ghost, only someone playing the role."

The companion's brown-eyed gaze darted nervously to each of the three who'd intruded into her bedchamber, but she gave no response to the explanation.

Roderick, an angry glint still in his eyes, looked around the room. He suspiciously asked, "Did no other person enter before me?"

As Miss Hartman hotly denied there had been any other intruder that night, she angrily tugged her blankets tighter around her as if she thought the soldier still harbored hopes to steal her virtue.

Elizabeth suddenly spotted the corner of a dusty sheet extending from under the edge of the lady's covers, an odd circumstance for such a neat woman. Without commenting she reached down and pulled the dirty linen free.

Silence reigned in the bedchamber as Elizabeth raised the sheet to reveal two large eye holes cut into the material, then stitched over with a thin layer of sheer white gauze. "Why, Miss Hartman, *you* are our ghost!"

A look of abject horror filled Miss Hartman's face. "I-I . . . oh-h-h-h . . . no-o-o-o . . ." The lady covered her face with her blankets, her distress was so great.

Roderick glared at the older lady. "Why?"

Instead of giving an answer, Miss Hartman suddenly tossed back the covers and leapt from her bed. As she rushed to the door in her nightgown, white stockings and brown half boots were clearly evident. "Go away! All of you, just go away and leave me alone!"

The hysterical woman tore open the chamber door and disappeared into the hall, leaving the three remaining occupants of the room in stunned silence as her footsteps hammered down the corridor. Her shrieked cries slowly faded into the distance.

At last Elizabeth gazed into Roderick's bemused face and broke the silence. "I should never have guessed Miss Hartman was our masquerading ghost. She is such a stickler for propriety."

Roderick's thoughts were momentarily diverted as he noted the way the light played on Elizabeth's hair, curling about the wilting white rosebuds. He preferred the way it had looked in the cellar, tumbled down about her shoulders. Remembering his anger at the brigand responsible for them being there, he was struck by a thought. Would the timorous Miss Hartman have hired the ruffian who'd threatened the woman he loved? "Something is not right here."

Julia, nodding her head in agreement, came to stand beside her friend. "I know what you mean, sir. This is not something Miss Hartman would have done on her own. Her reaction on being discovered was excessive. I think someone forced her to play our ghost."

Roderick drew his gaze from Elizabeth, whose mere presence held the power to distract him. "Then I think we need to find where the lady has gone, for I am certain she went to inform her coconspirator that the game is finished."

He ushered the ladies into the hall in search of Miss Hartman and answers.

"I told you I did not want to do this! Going to Miss Powers's room was so wicked!" Prudence Hartman paced in front of the settee on which Esmé sat in her bedchamber.

The heiress still wore her violet silk gown from dinner. As her companion marched before her, Esmé attempted to restrain the growling Reynard with one hand while clutching her amber-topped cane with the other.

During Prudence's frantic dash down the hall, the companion's favorite nightcap had been lost. Her frizzing hair fluffed around her head like a cloud of thick grey smoke. At this exact moment, she bore a strong resemblance to an escapee of Bedlam.

"I know, my dear, but how else was I to find which of the young ladies had the courage and the quickness of mind needed to take over an estate like Langley as well as my other properties." Esmé observed her companion with compassion. She knew she'd asked a lot of the strictly raised woman, but she'd had good reason.

Struggling to quiet her agitated dog, Esmé was struck by a peculiarity in what Prudence had imparted. "I thought you were to visit Myra's room tonight. Imogene and Julia have exhibited fortitude aplenty."

"I went there first, but the girl was not abed, so I decided to go to Miss Powers's room instead." The companion began to pace faster as memories of the event returned, making her thin face redden with embarrassment. "Oh, it was dreadful! When the major stepped out of the wall panel, I thought I would die of fright. Then he found the passageway to my room. They know 'twas I under the sheet. I am mortified."

Reynard gave a sharp bark as the lady passed his position. In such a state of distress, Prudence quite forgot her fear and snapped, "Oh, do shut up, you annoying little beast."

The fox terrier was surprised into silence by the lady's unusual lack of terror. As if he realized there was no more fun to be had in this quarter, he settled down on his mistress's lap and simply tolerated the intrusion.

Oblivious to the dog's change in demeanor, Miss Hartman continued to pace. "I shall never be able to face them again. My only consolation is that Mr. Tyler shall never hear of this dreadful incident."

"My dear, I shall tell them you were doing it for me. You mustn't—" A knock interrupted the lady, and she called for the visitor to enter.

The door opened to reveal a hallway filled with people. It appeared the entire household had been awakened by Prudence's banshee wails.

Major Shelton, Miss Fields, and her cousin Julia entered the room. The servants remained nervously in the hall, hoping to catch a snatch of conversation to explain the ruckus. Esmé smiled tentatively at the entering trio. "And so we are caught at our little game."

Elizabeth was startled beyond belief to discover Miss Hartman here, of all places. Obviously their hostess was behind the false hauntings. "But why, Miss Langley?"

Before the lady could respond, Imogene arrived at the open door. Tying the belt to her white wrapper, her unbound gingery hair was a flash of colour against the snowy material. "What is all the noise?"

"Come in, my dear, you may as well hear my explanation since you are as much effected as the others." Esmé gestured for the girl to sit beside her, then called to a footman loitering about the door. "James, please go and find Miss Bradford. She has a right to be here, as well."

As the servant disappeared to do the lady's bidding, the jingle of a carriage harness and the crunch of gravel sounded, indicating a vehicle had drawn to a halt in front of the Hall. Looking up at the mantel clock which read half-past twelve, Esmé frowned. "Good heavens, who could that be at this time of night? Is Aegis about?"

"No, ma'am," called a junior footman. "Miss Hartman shrieked loud enough to wake the dead, but it weren't loud enough to wake Mr. Aegis. I'll see to the door, ma'am," the young servant offered and disappeared to perform the duty.

Roderick, impatient to know why Miss Langley had engaged in such pranks, and little affected by who had arrived, replied, "While we await your midnight visitor, madam, perhaps you can give us an explanation for why you had Miss Hartman skulking around as a ghost?"

Esmé's companion blushed deeply and turned to the window. The lady's shoulders sagged with misery as she stood with her back to the people she'd tormented.

Feeling a twinge of guilt, Esmé eyed Prudence's cringing figure. "Allow me to say that Miss Hartman acted very much against her better judgment. 'Twas I who insisted she engage in such a trick, for I needed to know who among you had the necessary qualities to be my heiress. Courage and a good heart were what I was seeking, and I am pleased to say that both Julia and Imogene exhibited both."

The mentioned ladies exchanged puzzled glances, before Julia said, "But, Cousin, we both were terrified when confronted with your ghost."

"True, but neither of you ran away, and I was delighted to discover that both of you had the courage to defy my wishes this morning and go on searching for the missing pair. That proved to me you know what truly matters. You risked your chance at my legacy to follow your consciences. Money was not your primary concern. Your thoughts were rightly on those you love." Esmé smiled at the stunned faces watching her.

Roderick was filled with a sense of outrage. They'd all been played with as a cat toys with mice simply to prove their character or lack thereof. A foolish game which would forever alter some of their lives. "Miss Langley, while I can overlook your simple pranks here at the Hall, there can be no excuse for what you put Miss Fields through by having that man take us hostage."

Esmé's eyes grew wide as she shook her head in denial. "Major Shelton, I vow to you that I know nothing of that dastardly occurrence. I was as surprised as the others when it happened. Let me assure you, what I had Prudence do, while not strictly proper, was necessary to my purpose and completely harmless. What happened to you and Miss Fields was unforgivable. I would never take part in such a dreadful stunt. Please believe me, sir, I am more sorry than you know that such should have happened to a guest of mine."

"Someone here at the Hall paid the man to abduct us. I insist on knowing the person responsible before we leave." Roderick was still convinced that Mondell was behind the plot in some way. Suddenly he realized the baronet was not present, despite the fact that every other member of the household had been awakened by Miss Hartman's antics.

Before he could comment, James reappeared at the

door with Mrs. Bradford right on his heels. The woman sniffled as the footman announced, "Madam, there is no sign of Miss Bradford in her bedchamber."

As the rotund widow in a puce wrapper eyed the company suspiciously, Esmé attempted to explain the strange gathering. "Come have a seat, dear lady. We are a bit topsy-turvy, what with all the unusual happenings tonight."

The agitated widow walked into the room, then collapsed into a mahogany saddlewing chair, causing Esmé to wince at the groaning of the piece of furniture. Dabbing at her eyes, Mrs. Bradford cried, "A horrible screaming woke me, so I went to make certain Myra was unharmed and she was not in her room. I *must* know where my daughter is."

Esmé took pity on the mother's distress. She, too, was puzzled. Where could the chit have gone so late? "James, take the remaining servants and search throughout the house for the young lady."

The maids and footmen scattered in varying directions, whispering among themselves. For several moments after the servants departed, only the occasional sniffle from the widow disturbed the silence which had settled on the room. Then the muted footsteps of the junior footman who'd gone to answer the door echoed down the hall. "This way, my lady."

Elizabeth and Julia exchanged a look of shocked disbelief when a familiar female voice sounded. "No need to show me to your mistress tonight, foolish man. Just find a bed for his lordship. He has recently been ill, and I never stay at posting inns when I can make the drive to my destination all in a day."

Moments later, the young servant stood at rigid attention beside the door. In his deepest voice he called, "Lord Powers and his mother, Dowager Lady Powers."

A sleepy-eyed lad of twelve with brown hair and clad

in a rumpled blue suit was led into the room by a tall, thin woman in a liver-coloured traveling dress and matching poke bonnet. The lady's haughty countenance scanned the watching faces until her gaze came to rest on her daughter's. A frown appeared as she took in Julia's wrapper. Without so much as a polite greeting to anyone, she snapped, "Why are you running about in your bedclothes, you foolish girl. I—"

Esmé instantly recognized the stamp of one who'd married above her station, then used ill temper and arrogance to cover her insecurities. The heiress deemed it time to intervene. "Welcome to Langley Hall, Lady Powers. I am Julia's cousin, Esmé Langley. To what do we owe this unexpected visit?"

Harriet, Dowager Lady Powers, eyed the Langley heiress closely. Her inclination was to continue to reproach Julia for her ill-judged appearance, but wisely, she directed her energies to turning Miss Langley up sweet. "My dear lady, how nice it is to meet you at last. Did Julia explain that Lord Powers was ailing and I was unable to leave on the day you requested? The foolish child, no doubt, forgot."

"You do your daughter an injustice. She did inform me you could not come due to the young lord's illness, Lady Powers. I am greatly surprised to see you, with your son's health so indifferent." Esmé glanced at the boy, but he appeared only fatigued and in no way infirm.

Lady Powers smiled, a strained grimace that looked almost as if it hurt. "Why, his lordship is much improved, and a most urgent matter arose that required I come."

Julia, looking at her brother's pale countenance, surprised even herself when she said, "Mama, whatever the news, you should have sent a message, for Edward is looking burnt to the socket. With your permission, Cousin, I shall find a servant to show him his room and see he is put to bed."

Before anyone could say another word however, Imogene Shelton jumped to her feet. "Send a message! Oh, dear. I forgot all about the message for my brother." The young lady dashed from the room, but few paid attention to the girl, for all eyes were on Lady Powers.

Julia went to her brother, placing an arm around his frail shoulders. "Come, Edward, we shall see you comfortably settled. I shall bring you some warm milk before you retire, if you would like."

Harriet gaped after her daughter as she led the young lord from the room behind Imogene. The dowager had never seen her timid child so poised and unaffected. No doubt, the foolish girl thought to avoid having a peal rung over her head for her disgraceful appearance. The dowager turned back to Miss Langley, inspecting the woman from the top of her purple turban to her matching satin slippers.

Esmé smiled brightly, calling to Julia to show the young lord to any unoccupied room on the main hall and to get one of the maids to bring the milk.

Elizabeth was curious about the letter Imogene had gone to retrieve. She hoped it bore good news for the major, but her thoughts were distracted as she eyed the baroness. It didn't bode well for Julia that her mother had arrived. What urgent matter could have caused the woman to ride all day and half the night to reach Langley? Then a frightening thought entered her mind. "Lady Powers, has something happened at the vicarage?"

"Well you might ask, young lady. I believe your father has taken leave of his senses." The dowager rounded on Elizabeth, a frown increasing the lines on her once-pretty face, grown harsh-featured with ill temper.

Speechless for a few moments, Elizabeth didn't know what to say. "My father? Nothing is amiss with my sisters or brothers?"

"You must return home at once. I demand that you

convince the vicar and my hen-witted sister that it is the height of foolishness for them to be contemplating marriage. Why, she is two months short of turning forty and a confirmed spinster. They are making cakes of themselves. No doubt the entire village is laughing at them behind their backs."

"My father and Miss Lilian are getting married?" Elizabeth spoke more to herself than to Lady Powers, trying to comprehend the news. She grew quiet as the stunning revelation swirled in her brain. Her father remarrying? She was so taken by surprise, she didn't know how she felt about it.

Roderick stepped forward and put an arm around her. "Are you all right, my dear?"

Enjoying the sensation of being held by the major, she nodded her head, and tentatively smiled up at him. Suddenly, her heart began to hammer as she saw the tender look in his eyes. It was more than mere concern. Were her earlier hopes possible? Could he truly care about her? "I shall be fine. I-I am but surprised at the news, sir."

"I hope not unpleasantly so." His green eyes seemed to be communicating with her very soul.

Elizabeth suddenly wished they were not in a room full of people, so that he could take her in his arms the way he had in the cellar. Then she gave herself a mental shake. Her father was to marry Julia's aunt, this was no time to be thinking of herself.

Focusing her thoughts on Miss Wade and her father, Elizabeth realized they would be a perfect match. Their friendship had deepened after her mother's death, and her father had often sought the lady's advise on important matters. Even the letter from Ruth and Sarah had been full of praise for Lilian Wade. Elizabeth was certain her sisters must be pleased by the news. She was truly happy for her father's sake. "Not at all, sir. I believe they shall be very content together for they are very well suited."

Lady Powers's lips thinned in annoyance. "You are getting as foolish as Julia. I thought you would not be so caper-witted as to endorse a marriage by a pair who are well past the age to be deluding themselves with notions of love. I thought you would have more sense—"

"Mama!" Julia's voice cut through her mother's tirade. She'd been at the doorway for several minutes listening to the urgent reason for her widowed parent's late arrival, and she now realized that the lady had come for her own selfish reasons. It was clear she didn't want to lose her sister's unpaid services.

Like Elizabeth, Julia was delighted that her aunt and Mr. Fields would make a match of it. They deserved to be happy, but her mother, overbearing as usual, was determined to interfere. Finding unknown depths to her courage, Julia would not allow that. "I think you are overtired and need rest."

A look of outrage settled on the dowager's face. She stepped toward where the major still clutched the vicar's daughter. Glaring at the soldier, she snapped, "I shan't retire until Elizabeth Fields is packed and ready to leave in the morning. She must agree to do as I ask—"

"Mama!" Julia came forward and stepped between her mother and Elizabeth, her grey eyes meeting her mother's defiantly. "You are interfering with matters that are none of your concern. Aunt Lilian has served you well for many years. Won't you allow her a chance to follow her heart? Besides, I am certain Cousin Esmé can have little interest in two people she has never met."

Lady Powers shot an appraising glance at Miss Langley, who was looking at her with something akin to distaste. The dowager knew she would not be here risking her daughter's chances at inheriting the Langley fortune, had not the turn of events at home so overset her, she'd come to the one person the vicar might listen to—his own daughter. But clearly her efforts had been for naught, for Elizabeth didn't seem against the marriage in the least. Why the chit was positively glowing as she looked up at the dashing major who held her in a too familiar manner. But then the girl always had been a hoyden.

Straightening, Lady Powers cast an apologetic look at Miss Langley. There was little she could do here this night. She would go to bed before she did any further damage to her daughter's chances. "Pray, forgive my intrusion. I did not mean to disturb you with our problems."

Julia took her mother's arm. "Come, Mama. We shall leave Miss Langley to her midnight gathering."

Esmé suspected they'd just witnessed a daughter's assuming command for the first time in her life. Perhaps Julia's taking a stand about the search for her friend had taught her something about herself. Esmé was pleased, but she didn't want the girl, who was just getting a proper footing with her mother, to be browbeat. "Julia, will you please join us again after you have your mother comfortably settled? We have not finished our discussion."

It was clear by the expression on Lady Powers's stern face that she was somewhat confounded by the turn of events. She distractedly bid all good night.

No sooner had Julia and Lady Powers exited Esmé's chamber than Mrs. Bradford demanded, "Where is my daughter? Something must be wrong or they would have found her by now."

Esmé leaned over and patted the woman's plump hand. "The servants are searching, madam. They shall find her, wherever she has gotten to."

James fortuitously appeared at Esmé's chamber door as she sat back to wonder where the young lady had gone. As the footman came to stand before her, Esmé realized so many people had come and gone in her room that night, it seemed more like the lobby of Grillon's than a bedchamber. "What have you found, lad?"

The servant glanced briefly at Mrs. Bradford, then looked down at the floor as if flustered by what he had to impart. "The young lady is nowhere to be found, Miss Langley. We searched the entire 'ouse. What's more, Sir Gordon 'as piked off as well."

Mrs. Bradford lifted her bulk from her chair rather rapidly for such a large woman, her tone a near shriek as she asked, "Piked off? Do you mean he has left Langley?"

"Aye, ma'am. Sent one of the lads down to the stables, and the gent's rig is gone. 'Is valet is missing as well. Reckon all three is on the road." The footman took a step back as if he were afraid the widow might strike him, her face was such a mirror of outrage.

"Where can they be?" Mrs. Bradford collapsed into her chair again with a wail of distress.

Miss Hartman, who'd been quietly at the window, eagerly declared, "As I feared, an elopement!"

# *Thirteen*

Roderick and Elizabeth watched with horrified fascination as Mrs. Bradford shook a fist at Miss Hartman. "How dare you . . . you hatch-faced dragon! Don't you slander my daughter in such a way. Myra always behaves properly, unlike others who shall remain nameless." The widow swept the lady up and down with a disdainful gaze, taking in her nightgown, stockings, and half boots, as well as the lack of a proper wrapper.

Prudence, having been the soul of propriety her entire life except for Esmé's prank, wasn't likely to let a tongue-lashing from the likes of Mrs. Bradford go unchallenged. "So, you say, but the fact remains that your *proper* daughter is not abed where she should be, is she?"

Mrs. Bradford heaved herself from the chair, turning on Esmé's companion like a fighting cock about to engage in battle. Her round face took on the appearance of a ripe cherry. "I have no doubt she will soon be found and there will be a reasonable explanation. Myra knows what is expected of her. She would never throw herself away on a penniless baronet."

A spiteful glint glowed in the companion's eyes. "Perhaps, if you had been as interested in Miss Bradford's conduct as that box of sweetmeats tonight, you would have seen her cast sheep eyes on Sir Gordon all evening. But then, she has been setting her cap for one gentleman or the other since she arrived. I say the pair have eloped and—"

Esmé rapped her cane on the floor several times, causing Reynard to lift his head with interest. "Prudence! Mrs. Bradford! That will be enough! Nothing can be gained by these pointless accusations and speculations."

The widow quickly turned her ire on her hostess, completely ignoring the embarrassed looks of the major and Miss Field, who'd retreated to places near the door. Convinced that her daughter had gone beyond the pale, she gave vent to her frustrations. "I blame you, madam, for not sending that mincing fop away. What do you intend to do if he has abducted my daughter to Scotland?"

Prudence snorted, "Abducted? More likely the jade drove the carriage herself."

The two combatants again fell into a round of name-calling, ignoring Esmé's orders for them to stop. She shot a helpless look at the major and Elizabeth.

Roderick, taking pity on the Miss Langley, stepped forward. "Ladies!" His tone was so forceful the bickering women at once fell silent. "While the circumstances look telling, I suggest we arrive at no conclusion about an elopement without genuine proof. I propose the servants search further until we find Miss Bradford or some evidence to confirm that the pair left in each other's company. A letter, perhaps?"

"A letter?" Mrs. Bradford said the word as if she'd never seen or heard of such a document.

Elizabeth moved to the widow. She took the over-wrought lady's hand in a comforting gesture and edged her away from Miss Hartman. "I don't believe Miss Bradford would be so unkind as to depart without leaving a message for her dear mama."

Roderick gave Elizabeth a look which seemed to thank her for helping defuse the escalating fiasco. "Miss Langley, I believe that someone must look in both Sir Gordon's and Miss Bradford's rooms."

A bemused Esmé stroked Reynard absently. "The major is correct. We must know what happened to Sir Gordon and Myra. Prudence, kindly go search Myra's room for a letter."

Miss Hartman seemed to realize the magnitude of her ill-mannered conduct, for she hung her head and avoided looking at anyone as she hurried into the hall.

Esmé seemed lost in thought for a few moments, then said, "My dear Mrs. Bradford, I know you have been put into a stew by this, but I do assure you I shall see that everything is put to right."

Sniffling into her handkerchief, the widow wailed, "Just how might you do that, madam, if your cousin has ruined my daughter's chances by marrying her?"

"Mrs. Bradford." Esmé's tone became quite frosty. "The Mondell family can trace their bloodlines to William the Conqueror. Sir Gordon is young and foolish, but then so might one describe your own daughter. Whatever your thoughts on my cousin, he will be making your daughter Lady Mondell and moving her into the first circles of Society, a place she has seen little of from Cheapside."

Mrs. Bradford blushed, suddenly aware that Miss Langley had not been fooled by their name-dropping attempts to elevate their situation. Ignoring the lady's comment, she still clung to hope. "We still don't know that they have eloped."

"Major, would you take Miss Fields and see what you can find in Sir Gordon's room while Mrs. Bradford and I have a private chat? James will show you which chamber, and . . . I think you should search for more than a letter, if you take my meaning."

Roderick knew what he must look for—evidence of the

gentleman's involvement in the abduction. "We shall do a thorough search."

With a bow, Roderick escorted Elizabeth from the room, glad to be away from Mrs. Bradford's anguish. He cast a glance at Elizabeth as she trailed behind the servant. Like him, she'd been embarrassed by the altercation between the ladies. He suspected her own thoughts were more likely lingering on the news Lady Powers had brought. He hoped that knowing her father would remarry might soften her attitude about wedding him. She could relinquish her responsibilities, for her beloved sisters and brothers would now have a new mama.

Overwhelmed with the need to declare his love for her, he knew he mustn't rush his fences. Too many other things were distracting her attention just now. At least he'd gotten her to agree to a betrothal, and when the time was right he would convince her to make it permanent. He only prayed that she returned his feelings or else he wouldn't have a chance.

Following James down the dimly lit passageway to the east wing, Roderick came alongside Elizabeth. Instead of speaking of their betrothal which he wanted to be real, he concentrated on the matter which had sent them to the baronet's room. "I doubt Mondell was so foolish as to leave any incriminating proof that he was the one who hired that ruffian."

"I am certain you are correct." Elizabeth swept Roderick's frowning profile with a quick glance, before returning her eyes forward. For some strange reason, she was suddenly flooded with memories of his unromantic proposal in the meadow. She was only fooling herself that he might have feelings for her because her own were so strong.

Lost in her sad thoughts, she stumbled on the intersecting runners of carpet as they rounded the corner of the east wing. The major's arms quickly encircled her, setting off a wave of sensations which left her weak with longing.

As she drew out of his steadying arms, he remarked in a husky voice, "You are looking extremely pale, my dear. You have been through enough these past few days. I would not have you fall ill. We must speak of our betrothal but—"

"My lord," Elizabeth interrupted. "I am still as anxious as ever to know who was responsible for hiring that terrible man. I am not ill, only perhaps a little bemused by all the revelations tonight." She locked her gaze on the gold buttons on his soldier's tunic, not wanting to look into those intriguing green eyes which always drew her to him. Was he so anxious to put an end to this false engagement? An ache filled her heart at the thought of severing that slender thread that bound them, if only for a while.

Roderick touched her chin and tilted it upward, forcing her gaze to his. "Don't give Lady Powers's news undue consideration tonight, my dear. You are tired after all that has happened. Everything will be clearer in the morning."

Elizabeth's throat tightened as she fought back tears. She wasn't certain whether she felt like crying out of fatigue or because she didn't know what would happen to her now that her father was to marry. She was free to wed, but the man she loved only wanted her to protect her name. She pulled her chin from the major's disturbing grasp. In the morning she would release him from their betrothal, and she would be on her way back to Aylsham. Only her life would never be the same.

Not wanting to think about any of that, she said, "Shall we search Sir Gordon's room and leave other matters until this mystery is settled? If the gentleman has eloped with Miss Bradford, they surely traveled light. My belief is that if we search his belongings, we might find the match to the dueling pistol the brigand carried."

Roderick sighed with frustration as she walked away from him. She seemed determined to push him away. But he would not be so easily defeated. Once they knew where Mondell and Miss Bradford were, he would make her listen to him.

James, who'd stopped in front of the baronet's room, eyed the pair with interest. " 'Tis here you're wantin' to be, sir."

Roderick trailed after Elizabeth. As she entered Sir Gordon's room, the major paused beside the footman. "Did you know Mondell's man?"

"Aye, sir. Always kept me eye on the valet. Somethin' not right about that one to my way of reckonin'. Fellow loped off yesterday and didn't come back 'til near dark. Said he went to Harrowgate on business for his master."

Envisioning the disguised man in the woods, Roderick knew that the valet had the same height and build as the villain. The coarse speech had been misleading, but many could imitate such crude accents, especially one who'd spent time with those types. "I want you to go and search the man's room. See if you find anything out of the ordinary."

As the footman hurried down the hall, Roderick entered the baronet's bedchamber. Elizabeth had crossed the room and was inspecting the gentleman's belongings in the wardrobe. He restrained himself from going to her and declaring his love. Very likely James would be back in a few minutes, Roderick reasoned, not allowing him the time he needed to convince her to be his bride.

Seeing the intense look upon her lovely face as she inspected the articles on the shelves, he knew he must wait. She was determined to find the truth about yesterday. But he was equally determined to speak with her tonight, even if he was forced to declare his feeling during the cries of the cock at dawn.

His resolve set to win the lady he loved, he made his way to a Georgian dressing table to look for any communication left by Sir Gordon that might explain any of the mysterious events.

"There you are, Roderick." Imogene waved the crumpled note in her hand as Roderick and Elizabeth entered Miss Langley's bedchamber. "I am sorry it took so long, but Trudie discovered the letter when she cleaned my habit and she placed it in my desk drawer. I only just found it. 'Tis from Kirtland Grange."

Taking the missive from his sister, Roderick had little interest in what his uncle had to say. He knew the letter in his other hand was what Esmé and Mrs. Bradford were concerned with. "Miss Langley, we found this note in Sir Gordon's room addressed to you." He passed the sealed letter to the heiress.

Unaware of all that had happened in her absence, Imogene pressed her brother about his letter. "Roderick, the message came while you were missing. I apologize, but with all the excitement of finding you, I forgot to give it to you. No doubt it is from Uncle, gloating about his marriage."

Roderick frowned at his sister. "I shall read it later."

The surrounding group grew quiet as they waited for Miss Langley to open Sir Gordon's letter. Roderick scanned the faces of the company. Julia had returned in their absence and now stood beside Elizabeth. Both watched Mrs. Bradford with sympathy for her distress. That lady's hands shook while she dabbed at her eyes as she gazed at the cream-coloured vellum in Miss Langley's possession.

Esmé opened the note and read the contents. She

sighed, then dropped the paper to the settee beside her. The news her cousin imparted in his missive made all clear. Mrs. Bradford was right. Esmé was responsible for this foolish elopement. By forcing him to chose a bride before she announced her decision about the legacy, he'd made a rash choice and convinced Miss Bradford to elope. Why, only this afternoon she'd foolishly declared an elopement to demonstrate true love in her cousin's presence.

Filled with remorse, she wondered if she'd let her boredom overwhelm her good judgment. Had it made her forget that she'd been dealing with real human beings here and not just chess pieces on a board to be moved about at whim? Looking at the expectant faces, she said, "They have eloped."

Mrs. Bradford slumped back in her chair, shaking her head in stunned disbelief. A dazed look of despair filled her round face. "All is lost."

Elizabeth was filled with pity for the lady. The widow had clearly had such great hopes for her daughter. Elizabeth knew the kind of hopelessness the woman was experiencing. She'd known it on the meadow when she'd realized Major Shelton was offering for her out of duty. Impulsively she went to Mrs. Bradford, taking the lady's plump hand in hers. "I think Myra will be very happy with Sir Gordon. It was clear from their conversation that they have many of the same interests."

"Interests? One cannot survive on common interests, child." Mrs. Bradford sniffled into her handkerchief in such a way that Elizabeth was alarmed.

Esmé straightened, then rapped her cane upon the floor. "There is no need for such long faces. I have been such a fool, and I hope you can all forgive me. As I promised I shall set things right. I have come to a decision about my legacy."

The heiress slowly looked at each person in the room

before sitting back and stroking Reynard. "I shall divide my estate three ways. Myra and Sir Gordon shall have my town house in London since he already owns a neat little estate in Lincolnshire. You, Julia, shall receive Langley Hall and, dear Imogene, I shall leave you the estate near Brighton. Everything shall be split equally, and I shall have Julia and Imogene come to live with me. Introducing two girls to Society next Season shall be delightful."

Mrs. Bradford was suddenly all smiles. "Why, dearest Miss Langley, you have done just the right thing." In truth the widow had wanted it all for her daughter, but being no fool she would gladly accept the smaller portion—and feel grateful for that, after her daughter's foolish escapade. Besides, there was still the two hundred pounds she'd borrowed to dress her daughter for this occasion. Myra would be able to easily discharge the debt on her portion.

Elizabeth noted the frown on the major's face as he looked at Miss Langley. She knew the secret which prompted his reaction. Hurrying to him, she placed a hand on his arm and whispered, "No good will be served by telling them we found the dueling pistols in Sir Gordon's belongings, as well as the note. Myra would suffer for something she had no hand in."

Roderick looked down at her, seeing the pleading look on her beautiful face. He wanted Sir Gordon brought to task for what he'd done to her. But he knew she was right. There was little that could be done to the baronet which would not cause Miss Bradford to suffer. Allowing his gaze to drop to her alluring lips, he realized the sooner all this was ended, the sooner he could claim her as his true love. "I shall do as you wish and remain silent."

Esmé, who'd been receiving thanks from Julia and Imogene, eyed the pair curiously. "Is there some problem, Major?"

Tearing his entranced gaze from Elizabeth, Roderick

neatly covered their conversation. "Not in the least. We are both pleased with your decision."

Imogene, eyes sparkling with excitement at her good fortune, suddenly remembered the message from their uncle. "What is in your letter, Roderick?"

Smiling at his ever-curious sister, Roderick broke the seal. After he quickly scanned the missive, a stunned look settled on his handsome features. He dropped his hands to his side, the message still clutched in heedless fingers. " 'Tis not from Lord Kirtland but his solicitor informing me that the old gentleman died a week ago while attempting to follow his betrothed over a rather perilous jump. He awaits my instruction as the new owner of the Grange."

"You are the new viscount!" Imogene clasped her hands together with delight. The others stared in surprise at her improper display of feelings for a dead relative. "I know I should be sad my uncle has died, but I did not know him at all. Besides, we were badly treated at the hands of that gentleman, and I shall not play the hypocrite and pretend to mourn him. I shall instead rejoice at my brother's good fortune."

With a sinking feeling, Elizabeth realized the man she loved was now a viscount. He could look in the highest reaches of Society for a wife. He might still try to honour their mock betrothal out of a sense of duty, but she loved him too much to hold him. He deserved to wed some beautiful, wealthy lady, not be forced into a marriage for propriety's sake.

As the assembled group congratulated the new Lord Kirtland, Elizabeth slipped quietly from the room. Only Roderick noted her departure, but he could not free himself from his sister's delighted clutch and Miss Langley's eager questions.

\* \* \*

Elizabeth felt all thumbs as she tiredly removed the wilted roses from her hair. She knew there would be little chance she would sleep that night, so she determined to pack her belongings before she got into bed.

Tossing the last hairpin to the dressing table, she pulled the brush through her tangled curls. Her reflection in the mirror reminded her of herself at twelve with her hair loose about her shoulders. If only she could go back to a time when there was only carefree innocence and not the pain of being in love with a man who didn't return those feelings.

Determined not to sink into a mire of self-pity, she tossed the brush down among the pins and went to her wardrobe to pack. She pulled the door open, then halted when a scratching sounded from the hall.

Her knees began to tremble, when Roderick called through the door. "I must speak with you tonight, Elizabeth. Are you dressed?"

"I am, my lord, but it is too late—"

Elizabeth's attempt to forestall the meeting was useless. Roderick boldly threw open her chamber door, and they stood gazing at one another, transfixed in that moment of time.

She could feel the pounding of blood in her ears as she saw the tender but assessing look in his green eyes. He seemed a man with a mission, and there was a tingling in the pit of her stomach as he boldly raked her with his gaze.

At the sound of a door closing somewhere down the hall, the spell broke. Lord Kirtland advanced on Elizabeth the way his unit had moved on the French at Badajoz, relentlessly. When he was but inches away, he took her face in his hands, forcing her to look into his eyes. "Elizabeth Fields! I have you alone at last. Your friend and my sister are now settled here at Langley Hall, and there are no further distractions. Will you listen to me?"

Elizabeth simply nodded her head, too breathless at his nearness to speak.

"I love you! I knew it the moment I kissed you in that cellar. You are stubborn, reckless, and totally unconventional, but you are the only woman I could spend my life with."

Roderick could restrain himself no longer. He lowered his lips to hers, covering her mouth hungrily. It seemed like a lifetime since he'd last kissed her, his need was so great to feel those warm lips eagerly meeting his own.

Elizabeth's heart soared even as a wave of tingling sensations surged through her while she returned his embrace. He loved her. Nothing else seemed to matter at that moment, only the feel of his demanding lips possessing hers.

A gasp echoed in the hallway, interrupting Roderick and Elizabeth. Reluctantly releasing the lady, the major turned to the intruder. There, standing in the portal, Miss Hartman trembled with indignation. "I was right, you fiend . . . you debaucher of innocence. You can fool Esmé with your charming manners, but not I. You cannot say you have not been duly warned, Miss Fields."

"Ah, the ever suspicious Miss Hartman." Roderick marched to the door, causing Miss Hartman to back nervously away. "Go 'haunt' someone else, madam!" So saying, he slammed the door in the interfering woman's outraged face.

Upon returning to take Elizabeth in his arms, he noted the look on her lovely face. "Very well, I shall duly apologize to the old harridan tomorrow, but you must own she deserved the set-down for her unfair opinion of me from the first."

Elizabeth laughed, she was so blissfully happy. "I will own such, my lord."

Roderick's arms tightened around her. "Now that I

have gotten rid of that distraction, you must say the words I have longed to hear."

"I love you," Elizabeth said shyly.

He crushed her to him, his voice a husky whisper, "And will you at last agree to marry me, my dear one?"

A shadow appeared in Elizabeth's eyes. "My lord, you could look much higher for a proper wife. I am not certain I can be a fitting viscountess with my unconventional ways."

Roderick brushed a kiss, soft as a butterfly's wings, upon her trembling lips. "I want you, Elizabeth, not some safe and proper miss who might drive me to distraction inside of a week. I wish only to spend a lifetime loving you and filling your life with more excitement than you ever imagined."

Seeing the hungry look in Roderick's eyes, Elizabeth blushed, saying, "Then I shall marry you," before surrendering to the searingly intense kiss of the man she loved and who loved her in return.

After a long time, they drew apart staring at one another with besotted gazes. Elizabeth, still unable to believe her good fortune, hopefully asked, "After we are married, say you will take me with you on your return to Portugal? I could not bear to be parted from you for so long."

Roderick shook his head. "I shall have to sell out, dearest, for my responsibilities demand I take up the reins at Kirtland Grange. I fear I shall have only you to order about as I once did my recruits."

Elizabeth gave a mock salute. "Then, to please you, I shall obey your every order, my lord."

The viscount laughed. "That will happen only in my dreams, for I know you, my dear. But I wouldn't have it any other way, my darling unconventional love." He again drew her into his embrace, knowing he'd found his true love.

## *About the Author*

Lynn Collum lives with her family in De Land, Florida. She is the author of two Zebra regency romances: *A GAME OF CHANCE* and *ELIZABETH AND THE MAJOR*. Lynn is currently working on a novella which will appear in Zebra's Christmas regency anthology, *CHRISTMAS KITTENS* (to be published in November 1997). Lynn loves hearing from readers, and you may write to her at P.O. Box 478, De Land FL, 32724. Please include a self-addressed stamped envelope if you wish a response.

# LOOK FOR THESE REGENCY ROMANCES

# WATCH FOR THESE ZEBRA REGENCIES

LADY STEPHANIE                     (0-8217-5341-X, $4.50)
by Jeanne Savery
Lady Stephanie Morris has only one true love: the family estate she
has managed ever since her mother died. But then Lord Anthony Rider
arrives on her estate, claiming he has plans for both the land and the
woman. Stephanie soon realizes she's fallen in love with a man whose
sensual caresses will plunge her into a world of peril and intrigue . . . a
man as dangerous as he is irresistible.

BRIGHTON BEAUTY                    (0-8217-5340-1, $4.50)
by Marilyn Clay
Chelsea Grant, pretty and poor, naively takes school friend Alayna
Marchmont's place and spends a month in the country. The devastating
man had sailed from Honduras to claim his promised bride, Miss
Marchmont. An affair of the heart may lead to disaster . . . unless a
resourceful Brighton beauty finds a way to stop a masquerade and
keep a lord's love.

LORD DIABLO'S DEMISE               (0-8217-5338-X, $4.50)
by Meg-Lynn Roberts
The sinfully handsome Lord Harry Glendower was a gambler and the
black sheep of his family. About to be forced into a marriage of con-
venience, the devilish fellow engineered his own demise, never having
dreamed that faking his death would lead him to the heavenly refuge
of spirited heiress Gwyn Morgan, the daughter of a physician.

A PERILOUS ATTRACTION             (0-8217-5339-8, $4.50)
by Dawn Aldridge Poore
Alissa Morgan is stunned when a frantic passenger thrusts her baby
into Alissa's arms and flees, having heard rumors that a notorious
highwayman posed a threat to their coach. Handsome stranger Hugh
Sebastian secretly possesses the treasured necklace the highwayman
seeks and volunteers to pose as Alissa's husband to save her reputation.
With a lost baby and missing necklace in their care, the couple embarks
on a journey into peril—and passion.

*Available wherever paperbacks are sold, or order direct from the
Publisher. Send cover price plus 50¢ per copy for mailing and
handling to Penguin USA, P.O. Box 999, c/o Dept. 17109,
Bergenfield, NJ 07621. Residents of New York and Tennessee must
include sales tax. DO NOT SEND CASH.*

# ROMANCE FROM JANELLE TAYLOR

ANYTHING FOR LOVE       (0-8217-4992-7, $5.99)

DESTINY MINE       (0-8217-5185-9, $5.99)

CHASE THE WIND       (0-8217-4740-1, $5.99)

MIDNIGHT SECRETS       (0-8217-5280-4, $5.99)

MOONBEAMS AND MAGIC       (0-8217-0184-4, $5.99)

SWEET SAVAGE HEART       (0-8217-5276-6, $5.99)